The Hotel Nantucket

The Hotel Nantucket

A Novel

Elin Hilderbrand

Little, Brown and Company

New York   Boston   London

Copyright © 2022 by Elin Hilderbrand

Little, Brown and Company
Hachette Book Group
1290 Avenue of the Americas, New York, NY 10104
littlebrown.com

First Edition: June 2022

Little, Brown and Company is a division of Hachette Book Group, Inc. The Little, Brown name and logo are trademarks of Hachette Book Group, Inc.

The publisher is not responsible for websites (or their content) that are not owned by the publisher.

The Hachette Speakers Bureau provides a wide range of authors for speaking events. To find out more, go to hachettespeakersbureau.com or call (866) 376-6591.

ISBN 9780316258678 (hardcover) / 9780316445610 (large print) / 9780316471466 (Canadian) / 9780316487917 (signed) / 9780316487610 (Barnes & Noble signed)
LCCN 2021952578
Printing 1, 2022

LSC-H

Printed in the United States of America

For Mark and Gwenn Snider
and the entire staff of the Nantucket Hotel
with my love and gratitude

The Hotel Nantucket

1. The Cobblestone Telegraph

Nantucket Island is known for its cobblestone streets and red-brick sidewalks, cedar-shingled cottages and rose-covered arches, long stretches of golden beach and refreshing Atlantic breezes—and it's also known for residents who adore a juicy piece of gossip (which hot landscaper has been romancing which local real estate mogul's wife—that kind of thing). However, none of us are quite prepared for the tornado of rumors that rolls up Main Street, along Orange Street, and around the rotary out to Sconset when we learn that London-based billionaire Xavier Darling is investing thirty million dollars in the crumbling eyesore that is the Hotel Nantucket.

Half of us are intrigued. (We have long wondered if anyone would try to fix it up.)

The other half are skeptical. (The place, quite frankly, seems beyond saving.)

Xavier Darling is no stranger to the hospitality business. He has owned cruise lines, theme parks, racetracks, and even, for a brief time, his own airline. But to our knowledge, he has never owned a hotel—and he has never set foot on Nantucket.

With the help of a local real estate mogul, Eddie Pancik—aka "Fast Eddie" (who, for the record, has been happily reunited with his wife)—Xavier makes the savvy decision to hire Lizbet Keaton as his general manager. Lizbet is an island sweetheart. She moved to Nantucket in the mid-aughts from the Twin Cities, wearing her blond hair in two long braids like the younger princess in *Frozen,* and at the start of her first summer on island, she found a "prince" in JJ O'Malley. For fifteen seasons, Lizbet and JJ ran a wildly popular restaurant called the Deck; JJ was the owner/chef and Lizbet the marketing whiz. Lizbet was the one who came up with the idea for the rosé fountain and the signature stemless wineglasses printed with the day's date that became a social media phenomenon. Not all of us cared about Instagram, but we did love spending long Sunday afternoons at the Deck drinking rosé, eating JJ's famous oyster pan roast, and gazing out over the shallow creeks of Monomoy, where we spied the occasional white egret fishing for dinner among the eelgrass.

We all believed that Lizbet and JJ had achieved what our millennials called #relationshipgoals. In the summer, they worked at the restaurant, and in the off-season, they could be found scalloping in Pocomo or sledding down the steep hill of Dead Horse Valley or shopping together at Nantucket Meat and Fish because they were planning to cure a side of salmon into gravlax or make a twelve-hour Bolognese. We'd see them holding hands in line at the post office and recycling their cardboard together at the dump.

We were all *shocked* when JJ and Lizbet broke up. We first heard the news from Blond Sharon. Sharon is the turbo engine behind Nantucket's rumor mill, so we were hesitant to believe it, but then Love Robbins at Flowers on Chestnut confirmed that Lizbet *sent back* a bouquet of roses that JJ had ordered. Eventually the story came out: At the Deck's closing party back in September, Lizbet had discovered 187 sexually explicit texts that JJ had sent to their wine rep, Christina Cross.

Lizbet was, according to some, *desperate* to reinvent herself—and Xavier Darling provided a way. We wished her well, but the once-grand Hotel Nantucket had a tattered reputation to repair (along with the roof, windows, floors, walls, and sinking foundation).

Throughout the winter of 2021 and into the early spring of 2022, we watch local contractors, architects, and interior designer Jennifer Quinn entering and leaving the hotel—but every single employee has been sworn to secrecy about what's going on inside. There are whispers that our favorite fitness instructor, Yolanda Tolentino, has been hired to run the wellness center and that Xavier Darling is looking for someone with an "island pedigree" to operate the hotel's new bar. We see Lizbet Keaton come and go, but when Blond Sharon bumps into Lizbet in the vehicle-inspection line at Don Allen Ford—Lizbet in her Mini Cooper and Sharon in her G-Wagon—and asks how the hotel is coming along, Lizbet changes the subject to Sharon's children. (Sharon has no interest in talking about her children; they've just become teenagers.)

Jordan Randolph, the editor of the *Nantucket Standard,* ignores the first two calls he gets from Lizbet Keaton telling him the interior of the hotel is finished and asking if he would like a "behind-the-scenes first look." Jordan is one of the skeptics. He can't stand the idea of someone like Xavier Darling—a business titan from overseas—buying a historically significant property like the Hotel Nantucket. (Jordan is aware that Herman Melville wrote *Moby-Dick* before he ever visited the island. Does that make him feel any better? Not really.) But, Jordan reasons, if not Xavier Darling, then who? The place has been left to rot. Even the Nantucket Historical Association has deemed the hotel too big (and expensive) a project to take on.

When Lizbet calls the third time, Jordan answers the phone and reluctantly agrees to send a reporter.

Home and Lifestyle editor Jill Tananbaum is *obsessed* with interior design, as anyone who checks her Instagram will immediately realize (@ashleytstark, @elementstyle, @georgantas.design). Jill would love to use this job at the *Nantucket Standard* as a stepping-stone to a position at *Domino* or even *Architectural Digest*. Covering the renovation of the Hotel Nantucket could be just the way to do it. She's not going to leave out a single detail.

As soon as Jill steps through the grand front doors, her jaw drops. Hanging from the vaulted ceiling of the lobby is the skeleton of an antique whaling boat that has been ingeniously repurposed into a statement chandelier. The ceiling's beams, salvaged from the original structure, lend the room a sense of history. There are double-wide armchairs upholstered in hydrangea blue (which Jill soon learns is the hotel's signature color), suede tufted ottomans, and low tables that tastefully display books and games (backgammon, checkers, and four marble chess sets). The far corner of the room is anchored by a white baby grand piano. On the large wall next to the front desk hangs an enormous James Ogilvy photograph of the Atlantic off Sankaty Head that succeeds in bringing the ocean into the hotel.

Wow, Jill thinks. *Just...wow*. Her hand is itching to reach for her phone but Lizbet told her that, for the time being, photos are forbidden.

Lizbet gives Jill a tour of the guest rooms and suites. Local artist Tamela Cornejo has hand-painted the ceiling of each room with a mural of the Nantucket night sky. The light fixtures—glass spheres wrapped in brass chain link—evoke buoys and ropes. And the beds—*Excuse me, the beds!* Jill thinks. The beds have canopies fashioned from driftwood and thick nautical rope. They're a custom size—emperor—and they have ethereal white sheers hanging at the sides.

The bathrooms are the most spectacular Jill has ever seen in real life. Each one has a shower tiled with oyster shells, a hatbox toilet in a separate water closet, and a slipper tub, the base of which is painted the hotel's signature hydrangea blue.

"But the secret to success for any bathroom," Lizbet says to Jill, "isn't how *it* looks; it's how it makes the *guest* look." She flips a switch. Surrounding the long rectangular mirror over the double vanity is a soft halo light. "See how flattering?"

Jill and Lizbet gaze at themselves in the mirror like a couple of teenagers. *It's true,* Jill thinks; she has never looked dewier than she does standing in the bathroom of suite 217.

Then—then!—Lizbet tells Jill about the complimentary minibar. "I can't count the times I've been in a hotel room and just wanted a glass of wine and a salty snack, but being charged seventy dollars for a bottle of chardonnay and sixteen dollars for a pack of peanuts is offensive when I've already paid so much for the room. So our minibars will be stocked with a thoughtfully curated selection of Nantucket-sourced products"—she mentions Cisco beers, Triple Eight vodka, and smoked bluefish pâté from 167 Raw—"and everything is free, replenished every three days."

Free minibar! Jill writes in her notes. *Nantucket products!* Jordan should give her article front-page placement for this announcement alone.

Lizbet leads Jill out back to see the pools. One is a sprawling family affair with cascading waterfalls. ("There will be lemonade and fresh-baked cookies served every day at three," Lizbet says.) The second pool is an adults-only sanctuary, a teal-blue lozenge surrounded by gray-shingled walls that will be covered with pale pink climbing roses in the height of summer. Around the pool are "the most comfortable chaise longues in the known world, extra-wide and easy to adjust," and stacks of custom-ordered Turkish cotton towels in hydrangea blue.

Next, it's off to the yoga studio. Jill has never been to Bali, but she *has* read *Eat, Pray, Love,* so she appreciates the aesthetic. The ceiling of the studio is an elaborate teak carving salvaged from a temple in Ubud. (Jill considers how much it must have cost to ship and install such a ceiling...*mind-exploding emoji!*) There's a gurgling stone fountain in the form of the somewhat terrifying face of the god Brahma that empties into a trough of river stones. The light from outside is diffused through rice-paper shades, and gamelan music plays over the sound system. *All in all,* Jill thinks, *the new yoga studio will be an idyllic place to find a child's pose.*

But as far as Jill is concerned, the ultimate reveal is the hotel's bar. It's a high-concept jewel box, a space painted Farrow and Ball's Pitch Blue (which falls on the spectrum between sapphire and amethyst) and a blue granite bar. There are domed pendant lights that look like upside-down copper bowls and an accent wall *sheathed in bright pennies!* There's also a copper disco ball that will drop from the ceiling every night at nine o'clock. There's nothing like it anywhere else on the island. Jill is gobsmacked. Can she make a reservation now, please?

Jill races back to her desk at the *Standard* office. Has she ever been so inspired to write a piece? She types like a fiend, getting all the details down—including the rainbow-hued Annie Selke rugs, the curated selection of novels on the bookshelves of the suites, the pin-tucked velvet stools in the new hotel bar—and then goes back over the piece one sentence at a time, making certain the language is as gracious and rich as the hotel itself.

When she finishes her final edit, she takes the piece to Jordan Randolph's office. He likes to read each feature article on paper and then mark it up with red pen like he's Maxwell Perkins editing Fitzgerald and Hemingway. Jill and her colleagues joke about this. Hasn't he ever heard of Google Docs?

Jill stands in the doorway as he reads, waiting for his usual "Outstanding." But when he finishes, he tosses the pages onto his desk and says, "Huh."

Huh? What is *huh?* Jill has never before heard her extremely articulate boss utter this syllable.

"Is it not okay?" Jill asks. "Is it...the writing?"

"The writing is fine," Jordan says. "Maybe it's *too* polished? This reads like one of those advertisement sections in the middle of *Travel and Leisure.*"

"Oh," Jill says. "Okay, so..."

"I was hoping for more of a *story,*" Jordan says.

"I'm not sure there *is* more of a story," Jill tells him. "The hotel was falling to pieces and Xavier Darling bought it. He hired local—"

"Yes, you say that." Jordan sighs. "I wish there were another angle..." His voice trails off. "I'm not going to run it this week. Let me think on it for a little while." He smiles at Jill. "Thank you, though, for going to get a 'behind-the-scenes first look.'" He uses air quotes, which makes him seem like *such* a boomer. "I appreciate it."

Privately, Jordan Randolph suspects that the Hotel Nantucket will be like a work of art by Banksy—after it is unveiled, it will shine for one glorious moment and then self-destruct. One person who agrees is a ninety-four-year-old resident of Our Island Home named Mint Benedict. Mint is the only child of Jackson and Dahlia Benedict, the couple who owned the hotel from 1910 to 1922. Mint asks his favorite nurse, Charlene, to push him all the way to Easton Street in his wheelchair so that he can see the spiffy new facade of the hotel.

"They can fix it up but it won't succeed," Mint says. "Mark my words: The Hotel Nantucket is haunted, and it's all my father's fault."

Mint is talking nonsense, Charlene thinks, *and he definitely needs a nap.* She spins his chair toward home.

Haunted? we think.

Half of us are skeptical. (We don't believe in ghosts.)

Half of us are intrigued. (Just when we thought the story couldn't get any better!)

2. The Fifth Key

LIZBET KEATON'S BREAKUP PLAYLIST

"Good 4 U"—Olivia Rodrigo
"All Too Well" (Taylor's version)—Taylor Swift
"If Looks Could Kill"—Heart
"You Oughta Know"—Alanis Morissette
"Far Behind"—Social Distortion
"Somebody That I Used to Know"—Gotye
"Marvin's Room"—Drake
"Another You"—Elle King
"Gives You Hell"— The All-American Rejects
"Kiss This"—The Struts
"Save It for a Rainy Day"—Kenny Chesney
"I Don't Wanna Be in Love"—Good Charlotte
"Best of You"—Foo Fighters
"Rehab"—Rihanna
"Better Now"—Post Malone
"Forget You"—CeeLo Green
"Salt"—Ava Max
"Go Your Own Way"—Fleetwood Mac

"Since U Been Gone"—Kelly Clarkson
"Praying"—Kesha

Ever since her devastating breakup with JJ O'Malley, Lizbet has been searching for an inspirational meme that will make her feel better. She spent seventy-seven dollars at Wayfair on a framed quote attributed to Socrates: *The secret of change is to focus all your energy not on fighting the old, but on building the new.* She hangs it on the wall at the end of her bed so that it's the first thing she sees when she wakes up and the last thing she sees before she turns off the light.

All your energy. Not on fighting the old. But on building the new. The secret of change.

Easier said than done, she thinks. She spends all her energy fighting the old.

Reliving September 30, the Last Night at the Deck.

Last Night at the Deck is a bittersweet tradition—it marks the end of the summer season. Lizbet and JJ have to say goodbye to the team they poured so much time and energy (and money) into building. Some of the staff will return next spring, but not everyone, so a summer can never be replicated. This, they've found, is both good and bad. Last Night is a time of bacchanalian revelry for the staff. Lizbet and JJ throw down an excellent party, opening tins of beluga caviar and bottle after bottle of Laurent-Perrier rosé.

One of the traditions is the staff photograph that Lizbet takes of them all leaning up against the railing with the Monomoy creeks behind them. She frames these photographs and hangs them in the hallway that leads to the restrooms. It's a record of sorts, an album, a history.

Tonight's picture will be the fifteenth. She can hardly believe it.

Lizbet calls for everyone to gather, and they configure themselves into a creative and cozy pose. Shorties up front! Goose, the sommelier, and Wavy, the head server, pick up Peyton, who is everyone's favorite (and quite petite besides), and hold her lengthwise. Christopher and Marcus reach for each other's hands, their first public acknowledgment that they've become a couple this summer. Ekash and Ibo and all the prep chefs, dishwashers, and food runners fill in, finding their places.

Lizbet uses JJ's phone to take the picture because it's sitting right there on table 10 in front of her. She punches in JJ's passcode— 0311, her birthday—and his text messages pop up, all of them in an amusingly large font (JJ won't admit that he needs readers). Lizbet is about to click out of the texts when something catches her eye: I want you so badly. This is followed by Tell me what you want me to do to you. Lizbet freezes, but then she thinks, *Wait, this isn't JJ's phone after all.* It must be someone else's iPhone 13 Pro Max with an electric-blue cover and a photo of Anthony Bourdain on the back and her birthday as its passcode. A split second later— it's incredible how fast the brain processes even counterintuitive information—she understands that this *is* JJ's phone. These texts— she scrolls back until she finds pictures of a woman's breasts and what she knows to be JJ's erect penis—are being sent to and received from Christina Cross, their wine rep.

Goose calls out, "Take the picture already, Libby. This bitch is getting heavy!"

Lizbet's hands are shaking. What has she found? Is it real? Is this happening? Somehow she manages to play through (later, she will consider this a show of superhuman strength). She takes the pictures. They're good. They're the best ever. Then Lizbet takes JJ's phone and hurries to the ladies' room, where, sitting in a stall, she reads through the pornographic text messages—187 by Lizbet's count—that JJ and Christina have sent each other over the past three months, the most recent of which was earlier that night. Lizbet wants to flush the phone but she doesn't; she has the wherewithal to take screenshots of the messages and text them to herself.

Then Lizbet returns to the party. It's in full swing—Polo G is singing "Martin and Gina" at top volume, and Christopher, Marcus, and Peyton are dancing. Lizbet finds JJ in the corner at table number 1, the most sought-after in the restaurant, drinking a beer with a couple of guys from the kitchen.

"There's my queen," JJ says when he sees her. He places a hand on Lizbet's waist and tries to draw her in for a kiss, but she stiff-arms him, pushing his phone into his chest.

"I'm going home," she says.

"What?" JJ says. He takes his phone, and the texts from Christina brighten on the screen. "Oh God, no. Wait, Libby—"

Lizbet doesn't wait. She walks away, pushing past Wavy, who senses something is wrong and tries to stop her.

"It's not what it looks like!" JJ says.

Oh, but it is what it looks like, Lizbet thinks once she gets back to the Bear Street cottage she owns with JJ and reads through the texts one by one. *It's exactly what it looks like.*

The Hotel Nantucket is perhaps the only place on the island where Lizbet doesn't have any history or memories with Jonathan James O'Malley, so when Lizbet hears that Xavier Darling has bought the hotel and is looking to hire a general manager, she drives straight to Bayberry Properties to see Fast Eddie.

"What can I do for you, Lizbet?" Eddie asks as she sits down across from him. She has caught him during a rare moment in the office. Eddie prefers to be out buzzing around the island in his Porsche Cayenne, wearing his panama hat, doing deals. "I hope you're not here to list your cottage? Though if you are, I can get you an excellent price—"

"What?" Lizbet says. "No!" She tilts her head. "Why? What have you heard?"

Eddie clears his throat and seems uncharacteristically reserved. "I heard that you and JJ parted ways…"

"And?"

"And that you're eager to put him in your rearview mirror," Eddie says. "For good. So I thought maybe you were leaving island."

"Absolutely not." *If anyone should leave island,* Lizbet thinks, *it's JJ!* But she won't drag Eddie into their drama; anything she says will be mangled by the Cobblestone Telegraph. "I'm here because I'd like Xavier Darling's contact information." She sits up straighter and flips her braids behind her. "I want to apply for the general-manager position at the new Hotel Nantucket."

"You must have heard about the salary," Eddie says.

"No. I haven't even thought about the salary."

"It's a hundred and twenty-five thousand a year," Eddie says. "Plus full benefits."

Lizbet pulls back a few inches. Her mind lands fancifully on a trip to the dentist when she wouldn't have to worry when Janice, the hygienist, tells her it's time for a full set of X-rays. "Wow."

"I'm happy to give you Xavier's e-mail." Eddie snaps his fingers. "Didn't you tell me your father owns a hotel in Wisconsin?"

Lizbet's father manages a retirement community in Minnetonka, Minnesota. As a teenager, Lizbet used to pull numbers for the bingo games and escort the residents to their hair appointments at the salon. One year, she judged the butter-sculpture contest.

"Something like that," Lizbet says.

Eddie nods slowly. "Xavier wants someone with a background in luxury hotels."

Lizbet blinks. There is no way she can make the Rising Sun Retirement Community sound like the Four Seasons.

"But he also wants someone who has dealt with the Historic District Commission and the Nantucket selectmen."

"Me," Lizbet says.

"And who can charm the chamber of commerce."

"Also me," Lizbet says.

"The hotel has quite a tattered reputation to repair."

"Agreed," Lizbet says. "I assume you've heard the rumors about the ghost?"

"I don't believe in ghosts," Eddie says. "And I *never* listen to rumors."

Ha-ha-ha! Lizbet thinks. At least one of those statements is a flat-out lie.

"Xavier has his work cut out for him," Eddie says. "There's a lot of competition at the high end—the Beach Club, the White Elephant, the Wauwinet. I told him I wasn't sure there was another seat at the table, but he was adamant, and he does have deep pockets. The hotel will open in June, and according to Xavier, it's going to be the finest lodging this island has ever seen. But he needs the right person at the helm."

Lizbet nearly leaps out of her chair, she wants this job so much. "I'll send Mr. Darling my résumé tonight. Do you think you might…put in a good word for me?"

Eddie presses his fingers together in a way that seems contemplative, and Lizbet hopes he's remembering all the times he called the Deck at the last minute and Lizbet found him a table, even when they were crazy full with a wait list. Eddie always requested table number 1 and Lizbet granted that wish when she could (that David Ortiz was sitting there one night and Ina Garten another wasn't Lizbet's fault!).

"I won't put in a good word," Eddie says. "I'll put in a *great* word."

* * *

The next week, Lizbet interviews with Xavier Darling over Zoom. Although she thought she *crushed it*—dropping the name of the chairman of the zoning board to underscore her *local connections*— Xavier's demeanor gave nothing away. Lizbet figured someone like Xavier Darling would have a short list for the position that included people like the GMs from Wynn Las Vegas and the XV Beacon Hotel in Boston. However, only two days later, Xavier Zoom-called Lizbet and offered her the job. She was calm and composed as she accepted, but the instant she pressed the Leave Meeting button, she jumped up and down, victorious fists raised over her head. Then she collapsed in her chair and wept tears of gratitude.

The secret of change is to focus all your energy not on fighting the old, but on building the new.

Lizbet had a proverbial clean slate.

She visualized a Hollywood production assistant snapping shut the clapper board as the director shouted: *Take two!*

On the morning of April 12, Lizbet is, unfortunately, back to *fighting the old*—specifically, she's remembering how it was *Christina* who called her to explain away the sexting (*Those texts are nothing, Libby, JJ and I were only kidding around*)—when she gets a message from Xavier Darling; he's requesting a meeting. It's six thirty a.m.— Xavier, in England, is oblivious to the time difference—and Lizbet sighs. She was planning to get on the Peloton. But she has agreed to be at Xavier's beck and call, so she pulls a blouse on over her workout tank, drapes her braids over her shoulders, and fluffs her bangs.

Join meeting with video.

"Good morning, Elizabeth." (Xavier refuses to call her Lizbet, even though she has asked him to twice, telling him that the only person who called her Elizabeth was her late grandmother.) Behind Xavier, Lizbet sees Big Ben and the Houses of Parliament, a view so iconically London, it might as well be a Zoom background.

"Good morning, sir." Lizbet tries not to worry about his stern tone of voice, though she briefly wonders if today is the day the hammer drops and the hopes she has invested in the hotel will collapse, the whole thing a belated April Fools' joke.

"I'm calling to shed some light on things that might have been unclear."

Lizbet steels herself. What is Xavier going to tell her?

"You've never asked me—in fact, no one has asked me—why I bought this hotel. After all, I live in London and I've never visited Nantucket." He pauses. "Have you wondered about this?"

Lizbet has, in fact, wondered, but she chalked it up to her understanding of the very wealthy: They buy things because they can.

"I bought this particular hotel," Xavier says, "because I'm trying to impress two women."

Whoa! Lizbet pinches her thigh to keep from gasping. This is probably the only answer worth sacrificing her thirty-minute hip-hop ride with Alex Toussaint for.

"Two women?" Lizbet says. She checks her image on her laptop screen; she's maintaining a sort of straight face. Lizbet has, naturally, googled Xavier Darling. According to an article in the *Times* (London), he never married and has no children. The internet showed pictures of him at the Royal Ascot and the Cartier Queen's Cup with young, combatively beautiful women on his arm, but never the same one twice. Who are the lucky two, and will they both be coming to Nantucket? Because *that* will get the island talking! She would love to remark that buying each woman a private plane or a minor van Gogh might have been cheaper.

"Yes," Xavier says. "I'm going to share with you now who one of the women is."

"Wonderful, sir."

"One of the women I'm trying to impress is Shelly Carpenter."

Shelly Carpenter, Lizbet thinks. *Of course.*

"Do you know who Shelly Carpenter is?" Xavier asks.

" 'Stay well, friends,' " Lizbet quotes. " 'And do good.' "

"Precisely," Xavier says. "Elizabeth, I want a five-key review from *Hotel Confidential.*"

Again, Lizbet checks her image. Does she look incredulous? Yes—yes, she does. Along with eighteen million other people, Lizbet follows Shelly Carpenter on Instagram. Her account @hotelconfidentialbySC has become a national obsession. Shelly Carpenter posts at noon eastern time on the last Friday of every month—a ten-picture carousel of each property (she's rumored to take these photos with her iPhone)—and the link in her bio takes you to her blog *Hotel Confidential,* where she awards properties anywhere from one to five keys. The secret to her success is her witty, brilliant writing, her razor-sharp intelligence, and her refined sense of what works and what doesn't where hotels are concerned—but there's also mystery involved. Nobody knows who she is. The internet agrees on only one thing: Shelly Carpenter is a pseudonym.

Whatever her real name is, she travels the globe, reviewing the Hampton Inn in Murrells Inlet, South Carolina, with the same critical eye that she does the Belmond Cap Juluca in Anguilla. (Both received four keys out of five.) It's well known that Shelly has never given a five-key review. She claims to be on a quest for that elusive five-key property, but Lizbet thinks this is a feint. Shelly will never give a five-key review; withholding it is her currency.

"Well, sir, we'll try our best," Lizbet says.

"That's not going to cut it, Elizabeth," Xavier says. "We are going to *do what it takes* to be the only hotel in the world that woman deems worthy of the fifth key. We are going to leave no doubt in her mind. Am I understood?"

"Yes, sir, you're understood."

"So we *will* get five keys from *Hotel Confidential* by summer's end?"

A competitive spirit that Lizbet hasn't felt since she raced her brothers swimming across Serpent Lake in Crosby, Minnesota, surfaces.

Building the new! she thinks. In that moment, Lizbet believes she can achieve the (highly) improbable—no matter what obstacles she encounters.

"We will get the fifth key," she says.

3. Ghost Story

For one hundred years, Grace has been trying to set the record straight: She was murdered!

In August 1922, the *Nantucket Standard* reported that nineteen-year-old chambermaid Grace Hadley had perished in the fire that consumed the third floor and attic of the grand Hotel Nantucket—a fire that had been started by an "errant cigarette of unknown origin." Technically, this was true, but the article left out secret, salacious details that only Grace knew. The hotel's owner, Jackson Benedict, had set up a cot for Grace in the attic's storage closet, directly above his quarters, so that he could sneak up and "visit" her whenever he was in residence. In addition to her job as a chambermaid, Grace served as lady's maid to Jack's wife, Dahlia, who called Grace "homely" (not at all true) and "a smart aleck" (occasionally—okay, often—true). On Grace's very first day of work, Dahlia spewed bathtub gin in Grace's face, temporarily blinding her. (After that, Grace always kept a safe distance between them.)

Before the fire started in the small hours of August 20, Jack and Dahlia hosted a dinner dance in the ballroom, as they did every summer weekend. These lavish events often ended with Dahlia getting drunk and throwing herself at other men. The Benedicts would then repair to the owner's suite and scream profanities at each other; one time, Dahlia threw a silver candlestick that missed Jack but hit their tabby cat, Mittens. (Afterward, the cat walked with a limp.) Grace could only too easily imagine Jack whipping out their secret during one of these feuds, like a dagger from a sheath: *I'm sleeping with your girl Grace.*

That would have been all Dahlia needed to hear.

Grace was woken by the sound of sirens (faint though they were in the attic) and she smelled the smoke and felt the searing heat of the floorboards—it was like standing on a griddle—but she couldn't get out of the storage closet. Her door was jammed. She pounded; she screamed, "Help me! Save me! Jack! Jack!" Nobody heard her. Jack was the only person who knew Grace was in the attic, and he hadn't come.

Ghosts are souls with unfinished business on earth, and such is the case with Grace. She has tried to just "let it go" and "move on" to her eternal rest—but she can't. She won't. She is going to haunt the damn hotel until she has an acknowledgment of the hideous truth: Dahlia Benedict started the fire *intentionally* and then locked the door to the storage closet from the outside. She *killed* Grace! And Dahlia wasn't the only one to blame. Jack had seduced Grace, and the vast difference in their social status left Grace with no choice but to comply. Jack hadn't saved her. He was ashamed about having a mistress, and so he let her burn.

* * *

After the fire, Jack sold the hotel for a song—but Grace became determined to let people know she was still there.

She started with the eight-foot-high mahogany doors—termites.

Then the silks that had been brought back from Asia by Nantucket whaleships and the hotel's velvets, brocades, and toiles—moths, mold, mildew.

Grace suffused the hotel with the smell of rotten eggs. Management suspected the cesspool and called the plumber, but nothing could eradicate the stench. *Sorry, not sorry!* Grace thought.

When the stock market crashed in 1929, the hotel closed. It remained shuttered throughout the Great Depression and during the war, too, of course. These were, Grace admits, dull years. It was just her, the rats, and an occasional owl. Anyone who had heard the story of the poor young chambermaid perishing in the hotel fire had bigger things to worry about.

In the 1950s, a new owner marketed the property as a "family-friendly budget hotel." This meant threadbare sheets that tore as easily as wet tissue and waxy coverlets in obnoxious prints that disguised stains. Grace hoped that wherever Jack was, he knew how common and low-rent his once elegant hotel had become.

In the 1980s, when movies like *Poltergeist* and *Ghostbusters* came out and everyone was suddenly an expert in paranormal activities, it became chic to say the hotel was haunted. *Finally!* Grace thought. Surely *someone* would do a little digging and figure out what had happened to her. Grace started properly haunting the hotel guests who deserved it: the philanderers and the casually cruel, the abusers and the loudmouths and the prejudiced. Stories accumulated—cold drafts, knocking noises, a bowl set spinning on the server in the third-floor hallway, water falling drip by drip onto the forehead of a slumbering man. (This man was handsy with the girls in his office.)

The hotel was sold again, this time to a young couple who set out to renovate it "on a shoestring." Do such endeavors ever succeed?

This one didn't, though the hotel operated, sluggishly, into the new millennium. It next changed hands in 2007, sold to a man without taste (Grace had peered over the interior decorator's shoulder and saw plans for round beds and beveled mirrors). But the hotel never opened under this particular owner; he had invested with Bernard Madoff, and he lost everything.

After that, the hotel lay fallow and Grace again grew bored. During Hurricane José in 2017, she cracked a window, which caused a section of the roof to blow off and cartwheel down North Beach Street.

After the storm, the abandoned hotel's doors could easily be pried open, and the lobby became the site of many a high-school party. Grace received *quite* an education—she listened to the kids talk; she watched them pair off and head down the shadowy halls to find privacy in the guest rooms. She became a fan of their music (Dua Lipa, "Levitating"!). She learned about Instagram, Venmo, Tinder, Bumble, YouTube, TikTok—and the greatest platform of them all, Snapchat (the ghost!). Grace listened to debates about social justice and found herself growing impassioned. Every human being had dignity, even the maid/mistress kept in an attic closet!

Grace and the kids got along just fine until a girl named Esmé body-shamed a girl named Genevieve by posting a picture of Genevieve in her underwear in the gymnasium locker room. The next time Esmé entered the hotel, Grace's face appeared on the screen of her cell phone—her hair was still curly and dark under her white frilled cap, but her eyes were two infinite black holes, and when she opened her mouth, fire came out.

Esmé fainted dead away. When she came to, she swore to everyone that she'd seen a zombie on her phone; some real-life *Twilight* sh*t, she posted, a f**king ghost! A few kids googled *Hotel Nantucket* and *haunted*. But nothing came up; the digital records of the *Nantucket Standard* went back only to 1945. To get more information they would have to delve into the physical *archives*. The mere word evoked piles of dusty papers and more effort than they wanted to invest.

Grace had lost a chance to be recognized. And not only that, but the high-school parties came to an end and she was alone again.

Grace is, as the kids liked to say, hyped that a gentleman of tremendous wealth has bought the hotel and hired competent (and speedy) contractors and a decorator with impeccable taste. Grace zips around the first three floors trying to remain unobtrusive, though sometimes when she enters a room, an occupant will shiver and ask, "Did it just get cold in here?"

Grace is visible to certain people; she thinks of them as "the supernaturally sensitive." They can see Grace reflected in mirrors and glass, but most people see nothing at all. Grace can also pull off spooky-but-harmless manipulations. If she were to summon all her energy and strike out, she could probably hurt someone. (She fantasizes, of course, about walloping Dahlia Benedict, once on her own behalf and once for the cat, Mittens.)

In room 101, Grace catches a glimpse of herself in the full-length mirror that has just been mounted to the closet door and thinks, *No, this won't do.* Her long dove-gray dress and yellowing pinafore make her look like an extra in a Merchant Ivory film. She solves the problem of her dated outfit when she happens across an open box of the hotel's new bathrobes. They're white waffled cotton lined in a soft, absorbent terry cloth. Grace slips off her dress—naked, she still looks like a nineteen-year-old, full in both the chest and buttocks; she might even be considered "a dime"—and tries on the robe. It's as warm and delicious as a hug—and it has pockets! Grace decides to keep it. If someone caught sight of her in a mirror, what would that person see? Maybe a ghost wearing a bathrobe. Or maybe just a levitating robe wrapped around an invisible body.

Terrifying!

Grace is delighted by the thought.

When the new general manager, Lizbet Keaton, walks through the restored front doors of the hotel, holding a milk crate full of belongings, Grace thinks, *Finally, a woman in charge!* Lizbet is looking fit and sporty in yoga pants, a windbreaker, and a Minnesota Twins baseball cap that she wears over her blond braids. Although her face is as wholesome as a child's—she wears no makeup—Grace would place her age somewhere between thirty-five and forty.

Lizbet sets her crate on the new front desk and turns around, arms raised, as if to embrace the lobby. Grace sees bright sparks of grit and resolution flying off her. She is a person determined to succeed where so many others have failed—and Grace can't help but fall a little in love with her.

Hey there, Lizbet, Grace thinks. *I'm Grace. Welcome to the Hotel Nantucket.*

4. Help Wanted

Lizbet sets aside the third week of April to conduct her final round of staff interviews. She placed ads in the *Nantucket Standard,* the *Cape Cod Times,* and the *Boston Globe* and on Monster, ZipRecruiter, and Hcareers, but the pool of applicants wasn't as large as she'd hoped. Lizbet checked her junk folder but found nothing except e-mails from FarmersOnly.com (once, at a low point post-breakup from JJ, she'd made the mistake of visiting their website).

Lizbet doesn't mention the disappointing response to Xavier because day-to-day operations are her responsibility. She should be relieved she isn't inundated with college kids whose grandmothers will inevitably die the second Saturday in August. She doesn't need a *lot* of people; she needs the *right* people.

Grace is wearing her new robe and, to replace her frilled cap, the Minnesota Twins hat that she casually disappeared from Lizbet's gym bag a few days ago. She perches on the highest shelf in Lizbet's office, which gives her an excellent vantage point for seeing the candidates. Grace vividly remembers her own hiring in the spring of 1922. There were at least forty girls shepherded into the ballroom of the hotel, and each one was handed a rag. Mrs. Wilkes, head of housekeeping, had inspected each girl's technique as she dusted the wainscoting and the round oak banquet tables. Grace suspects Mrs. Wilkes had also been noting appearances, because it was mostly the pretty girls who were chosen; the ugly girls were sent home.

Lawsuits, Grace thinks now with a chuckle.

Grace peers over Lizbet's shoulder at the short stack of résumés on the desk. The first candidate is a twenty-two-year-old Nantucket resident named Edith Robbins who has applied for a front-desk position. Lizbet opens the door to her office and invites Edith— a young woman with luminous brown skin who's wearing a pencil skirt and kitten heels—to take a seat.

"Sweet Edie!" Lizbet says. "I can't get *over* how grown up you are! I remember your mom and dad bringing you to the Deck on your birthday."

Sweet Edie beams. "Every year."

"How's your mom doing? I haven't seen her since your dad's funeral."

"She's working full-time at Flowers on Chestnut and she took my dad's spot in the Rotary Club," Edie says. "So she's keeping busy."

"Please tell her I said hello. Now, I realize you're the child of two seasoned hospitality professionals, but I have to ask—didn't your mom want you to work at the Beach Club?"

"She did," Edie says. "But I thought this would be the more exciting opportunity. Everyone on the island is talking about this place."

"Oh, really? What are they saying?"

Edie gives Lizbet what might be called an uneasy smile. *What are they saying?* Grace wonders. Is anyone talking about *her?*

"Your résumé is *impressive!*" Lizbet says. "You graduated from the school of hotel administration at Cornell, where you were a Statler Fellow. You were number one in your class!"

Of course she was! Grace thinks. *Look at her!*

"In your opinion," Lizbet says, "what's the most important aspect of hospitality?"

"Making a genuine connection with each guest from minute one," Edie says. "A warm greeting and a smile—'We're happy you're here. Let us help you have a wonderful stay.'"

"Great answer," Lizbet says. "It states here that you worked at the Statler Hotel on Cornell's campus and then, last summer, at Castle Hill in Newport?"

"Yes, my boyfriend and I worked at Castle Hill together. That property is a-*maze*-ing!"

Lizbet's eyebrows shoot up. "Is your boyfriend here for the summer? Because I'm still looking for—"

"We broke up right after graduation," Edie says.

Grace can't imagine what kind of fool would break up with this captivating young woman.

"We both got offers from the Ritz-Carlton management-training program," Edie says. "But I wanted to spend the summer on Nantucket with my mom. Graydon asked if he could come and I said no. I wanted to start my adult life as an independent woman."

Good for you, Grace thinks. She would have wanted to be an independent woman back in the day if that had been a thing.

"I'd love to offer you a spot on our front desk," Lizbet says. "Your starting wage will be twenty-five dollars an hour."

Grace understands inflation, but even so, this number is mind-boggling. In 1922, she made thirty-five cents an hour!

"We're paying well above industry standard," Lizbet says. "But then again, we expect more. It'll be a rigorous schedule."

"Not a problem," Edie says. "One of the things they drilled into us at Cornell was that we would have *no* personal life."

"At least you're prepared." Lizbet leans in. "I suppose you follow Shelly Carpenter on Instagram?"

" 'Stay well, friends,' " Edie says. " 'And do good.' Her reviews are fire!"

Fire, Grace thinks. Everything good these days is *fire*. She can't wait for this term to move along.

"Do you think she'll ever give five keys?" Lizbet asks.

"My friends and I used to debate what it would take for her to grant the fifth key. The woman is *so* nitpicky, and yet she's not unreasonable. If you ask for skim milk with your room-service coffee, you should get it. The blow-dryer should work without pushing the reset button. I'm of the opinion that, if you pay attention and have the resources, then yes, a fifth key is possible."

"Excellent. The hotel's owner, Mr. Darling, is determined to get the fifth key."

Sweet Edie beams. "I'm *so* here for it!"

The next interview is right in Grace's wheelhouse: head of housekeeping! Grace scans the résumé: Magda English, age fifty-nine.

There are two addresses listed, one in St. Thomas, U.S. Virgin Islands, and one just around the corner on West Chester Street. Ms. English's experience includes thirty-two years as director of house-keeping on XD Cruise Lines. Ms. English retired in 2021, and yet here she is, the woman who might be the new Mrs. Wilkes.

Lizbet meets Ms. English ("Please," she says, "call me Magda") in the lobby, and Grace trails them down the hall at a distance; she can tell nothing gets past this woman.

"We have thirty-six rooms," Lizbet says. "And twelve suites."

Magda has regal posture and barely a single line on her face. As she and Lizbet stroll the corridor, she admires the mahogany barrel ceiling and the brass portholes, salvaged from a French ocean liner, along the walls. "I used to run housekeeping on cruise ships, so I'll feel right at home," Magda says. Her voice has a delightful West Indian lilt (whereas Mrs. Wilkes's voice had been like a cheese grater on Grace's backside). "These portholes will need to be polished every week."

Lizbet opens the door to room 108. Grace slips in and settles on top of the canopy bed, adjusting her robe for modesty. She's chosen this spot because she can't be seen in the mirror or window.

Magda walks over to the emperor-size bed and runs a hand over the duvet cover. "Matouk sheets?"

"Good guess," Lizbet says.

"I know my linens." Magda picks up the hydrangea-blue cash-mere throw at the foot of the bed. "This is lovely."

"All the rooms have them. They're woven at Nantucket Looms especially for the hotel."

"I hope they plan on weaving extras," Magda says, "because these will 'accidentally' find their way into the guests' luggage, I assure you." She pokes her head into the walk-in closet and then the bathroom. "How many people would be on my staff?"

"Four," Lizbet says.

Magda laughs. "That's a tenth of what I'm used to. But it should be enough."

"So what brought you to Nantucket?" Lizbet asks.

Magda sighs. "I spent the first half of my career on ships in the Mediterranean, then I requested a transfer back home to the Caribbean. When my brother's wife died in September, I took my retirement and moved here to take care of him and my nephew Ezekiel."

"Ezekiel English is your nephew? I'm interviewing him this afternoon."

"He's a lovely boy, as you'll see for yourself." She smiles. "Zeke and William have had a rough few months...but now that they're back on their feet, a little job will fill my days."

Lizbet raises her eyebrows. "This is more than just a little job."

"Well, it's not a cruise ship," Magda says. "My standards are impeccable, as my previous employer will attest. I promise you, the hotel will be cleaner than it's ever been in the past."

Well! Grace thinks indignantly. *I guess we'll see about that.*

After Magda departs, Lizbet considers going for a lunchtime run or grabbing one of the mountain bikes from the hotel's brand-new fleet and powering out a quick ride. This morning she finally felt a thaw in the air, but as tempting as it is to go outside, Lizbet decides to stay at her laptop. First, she checks the references of a married couple—Adam and Raoul Wasserman-Ramirez—who have both applied for bellman positions. They currently work at the Four Seasons in Punta Mita, Mexico, and want to come to New England for the summer. Lizbet has been putting off deciding about Adam and Raoul because she isn't sure hiring a married couple for the same job is a good idea, even though they both interviewed well over the phone. What if they bicker? What if one far outperforms the other?

The e-mail from the GM at the Four Seasons is glowing. It mentions that Adam has a "beautiful singing voice." (*How is this relevant?* Lizbet wonders. *He's going to be schlepping bags.*) The letter ends with *We at the Four Seasons Punta Mita have determined it's best if the Wasserman-Ramirezes are scheduled separately.*

Ha! Lizbet's instincts were correct—but the reality remains that she needs three bellmen, and her options are limited. She'll hire Adam and Raoul.

Next, although she has cautioned herself not to, she checks to see if there are any new reservations for opening week.

There's one, a booking for four nights made by a couple from Syracuse. This is heartening, but the fact that the hotel's overall occupancy is hovering at just above 25 percent a full week after the website went live is not. They placed banner ads on all the major travel websites, and Lizbet wrote what she felt was an excellent press release, but there have been very few takers. When Lizbet called Jill Tananbaum at the *Nantucket Standard* to see what had become of her piece, Jill said, "Jordan told me he might run it at some point but he can't say when."

Lizbet hung up, discouraged. The reputation of the hotel was, admittedly, abominable, and Xavier's interest in it was somewhat perplexing, but it had undergone a remarkable metamorphosis.

Building the new! she thinks. But only an instant later, she wonders if she's in over her head. It had been far easier to sell herself to Xavier than she'd anticipated (considering she had no actual hotel experience)—and only now does Lizbet wonder how much competition she had. Is it possible she was *the only person* who applied for this job?

Xavier has asked Lizbet to book him suite 317—historically, the hotel owner's suite—from August 24 to August 28. It feels a little strange that Xavier isn't coming until the end of August, but Lizbet is relieved. By then, she might know what she's doing.

Lizbet isn't sure where all this self-doubt is coming from; she's probably just hungry. She's tempted to run over to Born and Bread for a sandwich, but there isn't time. Her next interview is here.

The third résumé is quite impressive, Grace thinks. Alessandra Powell, age thirty-three, applying for a front-desk position. The very first line announces (in boldface) that Alessandra is fluent in Spanish, French, Italian, and English. She has worked at hotels in Ibiza, Monaco, and, most recently, Tremezzina, Italy. This draws Grace back in time. When Dahlia Benedict was being "nice" to Grace, she would gab about her and Jack's travels abroad. She told Grace that she and Jack had sailed to Europe aboard the *Mauretania,* and when Grace murmured sarcastically under her breath that it sure was a good thing the *Mauretania* hadn't hit an iceberg like the *Titanic,* Dahlia slapped her soundly.

It was a slap Grace deserved. By that point, Grace was so deep into the affair with Jack, she saw no way out. She very dearly wished the *Mauretania had* sunk with both Jack and Dahlia aboard.

Grace is yanked back to the present moment when a young woman with long, wavy apricot-colored hair steps into Lizbet's office.

No, Grace thinks. *No!* There's a stench coming off the woman that means only one thing: a rotten soul.

The woman, Alessandra, holds out a white paper bag. "I brought you an ABC grilled cheese from Born and Bread on the off chance you've been so busy interviewing that you skipped lunch."

Lizbet's blue eyes widen. "Thank you! That was so...*intuitive.* I *did* skip lunch, and the ABC is my favorite sandwich." She accepts the bag. "Please, sit. So, Alessandra, your résumé is nothing short of remarkable—Italy, Spain, Monaco. And you speak so many languages! What brings you to our little island?"

"It was time to come home. To the States, that is, though I'm originally a West Coast girl. I studied romance languages in Palo Alto—"

"Were you at Stanford?" Lizbet checks the résumé. "It doesn't *say* that here—"

"And then I did the whole backpacking-through-Europe thing—the train, the hostels—and I found myself flat broke in Ravenna. I went there especially to see the mosaics in the Basilica of St. Vitale."

"Mosaics?"

"They're the finest examples of Byzantine mosaics outside of Istanbul. They're magnificent. Have you seen them?"

Oh, please, Grace thinks. *How pretentious.*

"I haven't."

Alessandra says, "Well, when I say *flat broke,* I mean I gave my last euro as a donation to enter the church. Fortunately, I struck up a conversation with a gentleman who was also viewing the mosaics, and it turned out he owned a *pensione* in town. He let me stay for free in exchange for working on the front desk—and my career in hotels was born."

"So you were in Europe for…eight years, give or take? I notice there are some gaps on this résumé—"

"I wanted to leave Italy while I still felt fondly toward it. And I chose Nantucket because it seems like the most exclusive of the New England summer-resort spots."

"I'm curious…did Shelly Carpenter from *Hotel Confidential* review any of the hotels on your résumé?"

Alessandra nods. "She apparently stayed at Aguas de Ibiza while I was working there. Her piece was positive, but she gave us only four keys. She had a couple of legitimate complaints. The first was that the bellman took fifteen minutes to deliver her luggage to her room, which was ten minutes too long by her standards—"

"Oh yes, I know."

"And there was no salt and pepper on her room-service tray even though she'd specifically requested it."

"Ouch."

"Yeah, people got fired. You know that she wears disguises and uses aliases and always shows up at the busiest times, when the staff can't pay as close attention to every guest as they might otherwise. And sometimes she creates extraordinary circumstances to see how the staff reacts. Rumor has it that when she visited the Pickering House Inn in Wolfeboro, she slashed the tire of her rental car to see how quickly the staff would change it."

"I did *not* know that," Lizbet says, slumping a little.

"My advice would be to train the bellmen in basic auto repair, because I'm sure once Shelly Carpenter gets wind of this place opening, she'll make an appearance."

"You think so?"

"I can almost guarantee it. She seems to like Nantucket. She reviewed the White Elephant—"

"She gave it four keys."

"And she reviewed the Nantucket Beach Club and Hotel, which is where I'm interviewing next."

"You're interviewing with Mack Petersen?"

"I…*am*, yes. Mack has basically offered me a position already, but I told him I wanted to keep my options open."

Oh, come on, Lizbet! Grace thinks. *She's bluffing!*

Lizbet runs her finger down the résumé. "These references have only the main numbers for the hotels. Can you provide any names or extensions?"

"As I'm sure you're aware, there's a lot of turnover in the hospitality business. My GM in Ibiza retired and bought an olive orchard. My GM in Monaco got throat cancer and died." She pauses, milking the moment for all its worth. "Alberto. He smoked a pipe."

When Lizbet makes a sympathetic face, Grace groans. She would bet her robe and hat that there had never been an Alberto!

"If you call the hotels directly, they can pull up my performance records."

"You have the experience I'm looking for," Lizbet says. "High-end luxury hotels with a discerning clientele."

"May I ask what kind of pay you're offering?"

"We pay twenty-five dollars an hour," Lizbet says. "Though, because of your experience, I can bump you to twenty-seven fifty and make you the front-desk manager."

No! Grace thinks. She needs to get this little witchy-witch out of here. Grace blows cold air down the back of Alessandra's neck.

Alessandra doesn't even blink. Figures.

"The hours are pretty brutal," Lizbet says. "One and a half days off every two weeks."

"A day off? What's that?"

"Ha!" Lizbet says. "You're too good to be true."

Grace has a feeling this is precisely the case.

Staff of five, Lizbet thinks as she takes a bite of the apple, bacon, and white cheddar grilled cheese on cranberry-studded sourdough that Alessandra brought her. Alessandra interviewed well, though her résumé has holes in it. There's a recent year-long period that's unaccounted for, but it's possible Alessandra was traveling between jobs; she seems cultured, into art and languages. And she said she'd studied romance languages in Palo Alto—"Palo Alto" is a wink-wink reference to Stanford, but if Alessandra went to Stanford, wouldn't that be plastered across the top of her résumé? Lizbet decides to overlook these things. Mack Petersen down at the Beach Club basically offered Alessandra a job, but Lizbet snapped her up!

Alessandra seemed to know a great deal about Shelly Carpenter. Alessandra could be their secret weapon.

What an improvement! Grace thinks when she sets eyes on the final candidate of the day. Ezekiel English, twenty-four years old, is, as the kids say, a smoke-show. (It's another piece of slang Grace doesn't love, though she can see how it applies now. She's feeling a little warm in her robe, and she pulls open the collar.)

Zeke gives Lizbet a dazzling smile and shakes her hand. "Hey, I'm Zeke English, what's good?"

"The sandwich I just finished was good," Lizbet says. "If that's what you mean?"

"Sorry, I'm a little nervous," Zeke says. "Thanks for having me in."

How adorable! Grace thinks. *He's nervous.*

"Please, have a seat," Lizbet says. "I met your aunt Magda this morning."

"Yeah," Zeke says. "Aunt Magda's the bomb. She moved in with us last September..." Zeke bows his head, and when he raises it again, his eyes are bright with tears. He clears his throat. "My mom died of a brain aneurysm. Aunt Magda cooks for us and...just generally makes everything better." He wipes a tear with the back of his hand, and before Grace can stop herself, she flies down to give his broad shoulders a squeeze. She loves a man who isn't afraid to show his emotions. The hug seems to revive Zeke a bit (or maybe Grace is giving herself too much credit?), because he sits up straighter and laughs. "Am I blowing this interview or what?"

Lizbet leans forward. "I'm interested in hiring human beings," she says. "Not robots. You experienced a profound loss." She takes a breath. "Let's start over. Hi, Zeke, welcome! How long have you lived on Nantucket?"

"My whole life, born and raised."

"Where else have you worked on the island?" Lizbet asks.

"I've been teaching at the surf school out in Cisco since I was fifteen," Zeke says.

He's a surfer! Grace thinks. Well, it's official: Zeke is her crush.

She wonders if he would be interested in a ghost with the figure of a nineteen-year-old but the wisdom of someone *much* older. (She's kidding! The scene in that nineties movie at the potter's wheel would—sadly—never happen in real life.)

"That's a fun job," Lizbet says. "Why make the switch to hospitality?"

Zeke laughs. "My dad told me it was time to grow up. He said I could either work here or work for him. He was the electrician on this renovation."

"Yes," Lizbet says. "William and his crew did a wonderful job."

Zeke says, "I couldn't believe it when I heard someone was fixing it up. It had always seemed like a lost cause. You know, my friends and I used to party here in high school."

O! M! G! Grace thinks. Zeke is one of her high-school partiers all grown up!

"Some strange stuff happened this one night," Zeke says. "A ghost's face appeared on this chick's phone." He pauses. "So then this place got a reputation for being haunted, and we stopped coming."

Lizbet gives him an indulgent smile. "Don't worry, we did an exorcism when we renovated."

Ha-ha, Grace thinks. She considers floating Zeke's résumé off the desk to prove just how wrong Lizbet is, but she doesn't want to show off. Yet.

Lizbet likes Zeke—he's a lovely boy, just as Magda promised—though Lizbet worries he might be a bit surfer-dude laid-back for the job. What if it takes him fifteen minutes to get bags to a room instead of Shelly Carpenter's prescribed five minutes? She sighs. Women will go crazy when they see him...he's a dead ringer for Regé-Jean Page. And she's already hired Magda, and his father *is* their electrical contractor, so she can't *not* hire him. Lizbet will just have to train him and Adam and Raoul that bags go directly to the room within five minutes! And she would like to train Zeke not to mention the ghost to anyone. Can she get away with that?

She sends him a text: You have the job!

Zeke texts back: Kk.

Lizbet closes her eyes. *Kk?*

A second text comes in: Thank you very much for the opportunity. I won't let you down!

Lizbet exhales. She can work with that.

The last person Lizbet has to hire is a night auditor, but the only application she's received for the job is from some guy named Victor Valerio (real name?) who sent a picture of himself wearing white face makeup, glow-in-the-dark fangs, and a long flowing black cape. When you ask for people to work the graveyard shift, Lizbet supposes, you end up with vampires.

Perfect company for their ghost, she thinks, laughing to herself. She'll have to handle the night auditing until someone suitable applies.

She sends Xavier an e-mail.

> Dear Xavier—
> I hired our core staff today. Onward toward the fifth key!
>
> All best, Lizbet

5. Opening Day

June 6, 2022

From: Xavier Darling (xd@darlingent.co.uk)

To: Employees of the Hotel Nantucket

The day has come! We're finally opening our doors to the public to show them our living work of art. The thing that makes it "living" is all of you. What do hammered-silver basins in the bathroom matter if the staff is harried and distracted when you check in? What does the Swedish sauna in the wellness center matter if the bellman delivers the wrong bags to your room? Hotels are only as good as their staff.

I will be personally reading every review of our hotel on the TravelTattler website, and based on the content of that feedback, I'll be awarding a cash prize of one thousand dollars to the most outstanding employee each week. I hope each one of you wins, though be warned, this isn't a participation trophy. It's entirely possible, for example, that the same employee will win all eighteen weeks of the season.

It's my goal to make the Hotel Nantucket the undisputed best in the world. But I can't do it without you.

Thank you for your dedication and hard work.

XD

* * *

Lizbet pulls her cherry-red Mini Cooper into the space that says RE-SERVED FOR GENERAL MANAGER and throws back what's left of her double espresso. She's *livid* about the e-mail that Xavier sent out that morning. Xavier is going to award weekly cash prizes to her staff as though they're contestants on a reality show. Lizbet has spent the past two weeks training the front of the house, and she was crystal clear that putting forth one's best effort every single day should be *a matter of personal pride and integrity*. She also stressed teamwork, a concept that awarding individual cash prizes will unravel.

Two days ago, Lizbet stayed at the hotel as a guest. The staff was instructed to use Lizbet's visit as a full dress rehearsal. Front-desk manager Alessandra checked Lizbet in, and Alessandra presented her with the Blue Book, a compilation of Nantucket's best beaches, outings, museums, sights, restaurants, galleries, shopping, bars, and nightlife that Lizbet herself had spent countless hours curating, writing, and refining. Alessandra asked if she could make Lizbet any dinner reservations. No, thank you, Lizbet said, though she would like a Reuben from Walter's delivered to her room between seven fifteen and seven thirty. Alessandra said she'd take care of it, no problem. A few moments after Lizbet stepped into the room— only long enough for her to admire the view of Easton Street from the picture window—Zeke arrived with Lizbet's luggage.

Lizbet flung herself across the emperor-size bed. She wasn't at the Deck anymore, and she certainly wasn't at the Rising Sun Retirement Community in Minnetonka. She was the general manager of the new and improved Hotel Nantucket. The sheets were soft under Lizbet's cheek and they smelled vaguely, though not overwhelmingly, floral. The mattress was so comfortable that Lizbet closed her eyes and took one of the most delightful naps of her life.

The secret of change is to focus all your energy not on fighting the old, but on building the new.

She left a few tests for the housekeeping crew—a crumpled tissue kicked to the far back corner under the bed, a cake of the Nantucket Looms wildflower soap tucked incongruously behind the (complimentary) smoked bluefish pâté in the minibar. She even went so far as to empty the matches from the box by the bathtub into her suitcase. Would Magda's crew actually use their hundred-point checklist?

Yes, they would. When Lizbet investigated the room the following day, everything had been cleaned, replaced, refilled.

She had been eager to see what was happening down at the hotel bar—it was subcontracted out, so Lizbet had no say in how it was run—but she found the door locked and the glass front papered over. She could hear voices and movement inside but when she knocked, nobody answered. Lizbet had repeatedly asked Xavier who would be running the bar and he said he wanted it to be a "grand surprise." Apparently, he'd signed a "swoon-worthy" chef to prepare the bar menu, but he was keeping the announcement under wraps until opening day, which felt very cloak-and-dagger to Lizbet. She sneaked around to the outside door and noticed that orders had been delivered. A young woman popped out, startling Lizbet. She said her name was Beatriz, and when Lizbet asked who she worked for, Beatriz said, "Chef." And when Lizbet said, "Chef who?" Beatriz shook her head and said, *"No puedo decirte hasta mañana."*

Lizbet took a yoga class with Yolanda in the Balinese-inspired studio, and although it sounded trite, she emerged feeling centered and at peace…or as centered and at peace as she could feel with the hotel opening the next day.

When Lizbet checked out of her room, Zeke tucked her suitcase into the back of her Mini for the long drive home to her cottage on Bear Street, which was 1.2 miles away. Along with her bill, Lizbet was presented with a parting gift: a very cold bar of Nantucket Looms wildflower soap.

Lizbet knew it sounded ridiculous, but she wished she could stay. It had been luxurious, even though she was technically working. And she was pleased to report that there had been no scary noises, no cold blasts, no ethereal visions, no signs of any ghost.

The hotel sparkles in the June sun with its fresh cedar shingles and crisp white trim. The hotel's landscaper, Anastasia, placed lavish pots overflowing with snapdragons, bluebells, lavender, and ivy on each step of the staircase leading up to the hotel entrance. The wide front porch of the hotel is set up with wide rockers with cushions in hydrangea blue and cocktail tables that can be turned into firepits. (The front desk sells a s'mores kit for eight dollars.) The porch will also be the site of the complimentary wine-and-cheese hour each evening. Lizbet has seen to it that they will serve excellent wine and a selection of imported cheeses garnished with ripe berries and plump, glistening olives.

Lizbet checks for mascara on her eyelids and lipstick on her teeth. She stayed up way too late last night trying on outfits. It's a new job and she wants a new style. At the Deck, she always wore muumuus because they were forgiving (she averaged eight glasses of rosé and fourteen pieces of bacon *daily*). Now her closet is filled with things that are fitted and a bit more professional. Today she's wearing a navy halter dress, nude stiletto sandals, and a Minnesota Golden Gophers charm on a chain around her neck.

She steps out of the car, so excited she could *levitate*. She feels like a living, breathing inspirational meme. She has stopped fighting the old and started building the new! She's weathered the storm by adjusting her sails! She is a pineapple: standing tall, wearing a crown, and sweet on the inside!

Lizbet slips her phone into her navy-and-white-striped clutch and looks up to find her ex-boyfriend JJ O'Malley standing in the white-shell-covered parking lot with his hands behind his back.

This is not *happening,* she thinks. Lizbet hasn't actually seen JJ since the awful day in late October when he moved the last of his belongings out of their cottage. He told Lizbet he was spending the off-season in upstate New York with his parents; he'd gotten a part-time gig cooking at the Hasbrouck House. By that time, Lizbet had already accepted the job at the hotel, but she didn't tell JJ that. But clearly he's heard the news. The Cobblestone Telegraph is real.

"What are you doing here, JJ?" Lizbet asks. He's wearing cargo shorts, his Black Dog T-shirt, chef's clogs, and a green bandanna around his neck. A thought occurs to Lizbet that's so horrible, she nearly drops her clutch: the chef of the new hotel bar has been kept "a grand surprise" because, in the world's most hideous twist, Xavier has hired JJ.

Lizbet will quit.

No, she won't quit. She'll make JJ quit. But one thing is for damn sure: she and JJ O'Malley are *not* working in the same building.

"Are *you* running the bar here?" she asks.

"What?" JJ says. "No. I wasn't even approached. Why?"

Sweet lightning, Lizbet thinks.

JJ brings his hands out from behind his back. He's holding a dozen long-stemmed pink roses wrapped in butcher paper. He gives her what she used to call his puppy-dog look—big eyes and protruding lower lip. In happier days, this would spur Lizbet to squeeze him tight and pepper his face with kisses, but now she thinks, *Wow, he looks awful.* It was normal for JJ to let his hair and beard grow out over the winter, but has it ever been *this* unruly? His beard straggles across his face like creeper vines on a brick wall.

"First of all, I came to wish you good luck for opening day."

A text would have sufficed (though Lizbet blocked his number months ago). "You betcha. And I'm not taking those flowers. What else?"

He drops the roses to the ground, reaches into the deep flapped pocket of his cargo shorts, and pulls out a ring box.

"Don't you dare," Lizbet says.

JJ sinks to one knee on the crushed shells and Lizbet winces—but no, sorry, she's finished empathizing with this guy's pain.

He opens the box.

Don't look at the ring! she thinks.

But come on, she's only human. She crunches through the shells in her stilettos and studies the ring; it's a dazzler. It's either fake or JJ took out an enormous line of credit on the restaurant—a move she would have absolutely vetoed if they were still together. It's over two carats, maybe even two and a half, and it's a marquise cut, which is what she's always wanted.

"I had a lot of time to think over the winter," JJ says. "I love you, Libby. Marry me. Be my wife."

Lizbet is standing close enough to see a hole in the shoulder of JJ's Black Dog T-shirt, a shirt she knows he's had since the summer of 2002. It was his first cooking job, over on the Vineyard.

"The answer is no. And you know why."

He gets to his feet; his knee is encrusted with shells. "You can't stay mad forever."

"I'm not mad," Lizbet says. "And I'm also not going to marry you. You cheated on me."

"I didn't touch Christina," JJ says. "Not once did I touch her."

"That may be so," Lizbet says. "But clearly there was enough *electricity* or *chemistry* between the two of you that the mere idea of her gave you a hard-on that you then went to the trouble of *photographing* and *sending* to her along with *one hundred and eighty-seven texts* describing what you would like to do with her if you ever got her alone in the wine cellar." The espresso Lizbet just finished asserts itself; it's liquid anger coursing through her bloodstream. "You're a *cheater,* JJ. I will not marry you and all the forgive-me flowers in the world won't change my mind. You're a jerk for showing up here."

"What do I have to do to get you to forgive me? I can't run the restaurant without you."

"Hire Christina."

"I don't want Christina. I want you."

"I'm guessing what you really mean is that Christina was black-balled by every restaurant on this island—as she should have been—so she moved to Jackson Hole." Lizbet can only hope this is true.

"Libby, please, I'm desperate. I'm lost. And look at you, baby, you're a hundred times hotter than you've ever been."

For one vainglorious second, JJ snags Lizbet's attention. She has spent the months since they split running and riding the damn Peloton and taking private barre classes with Yolanda. She has lost thirty-two pounds, carved out the sides of her thighs, and scooped out her ass cheeks. She can wall-sit for two and a half minutes and plank for three; she can hold a crow pose in yoga; she has triceps! And today, she has freed her hair from the usual braids; she's wearing it sleek and long, parted down the middle.

Lizbet has been chasing something, and that something is revenge. She has been waiting for the moment when JJ would acknowledge her change in appearance. *A hundred times hotter*. It's a start. Far more important than how Lizbet looks is how she feels, which is strong, healthy, motivated! She's not going to drink eight glasses of rosé every night this summer, she's not going to share JJ's cigarettes or stay up until three in the morning. She's finished with that lifestyle.

"I need to get to work," Lizbet says. "Please leave and take back the ring."

"So you're saying you don't love me?" JJ reaches into his pocket again, and Lizbet suddenly feels panicky, afraid that he's going to pull out a gun and…shoot her? Himself? Is he *that* unhinged? She takes a step back but then sees it's just his phone in his hand.

"You're telling me you can listen to this and not feel anything?" He plays "White Flag" by Dido. *But I will go down with this ship.* How many times did Lizbet and JJ sing this at the top of their lungs in JJ's truck as they rode to the beach at two in the morning so they could see the moonlight on the ocean? How many times did they dance to the song in their kitchen? *I'm in love and always will be.*

Playing it now is unfair.

"What I feel is sad and disappointed," Lizbet says. "You betrayed my trust. You tossed fifteen years of my love down the drain because you couldn't stop yourself from telling Christina that you wanted to tongue her nipples."

JJ winces. "I never said that."

"Oh, but you did. Get out of here, JJ, before I have one of my bellmen physically remove you."

JJ puts the ring box in his pocket and straightens up to his full height. He's six foot five and weighs two hundred and eighty pounds. In the Land of Ten Thousand Lakes, where Lizbet was raised, that's called a Paul Bunyan.

"Or I'll get a restraining order," Lizbet says.

"Libby—" He grabs her arm and she wrenches it away.

"Is there a problem?" A man in a white jacket and houndstooth pants steps out of the entrance to the new hotel bar and strides over to JJ and Lizbet.

Who is this? Lizbet thinks. The script on his jacket reads CHEF MARIO SUBIACO.

Lizbet fights to keep her composure. Mario *Subiaco?* Almost involuntarily, Lizbet looks over at JJ. His mouth has fallen open a bit.

"I'm Mario Subiaco," Mario Subiaco says, offering Lizbet his hand. "The chef of the Blue Bar."

The Blue Bar. Of course—Mario Subiaco used to be the pastry chef at the Blue Bistro, which was Nantucket's best restaurant before it closed in 2005. Mario Subiaco is *the* OG Nantucket celebrity chef. JJ keeps Mario's picture—clipped from a profile of him in *Vanity Fair* that was written just after the Blue Bistro shut its doors—taped to his office wall! Lizbet thought Mario Subiaco was in Los Angeles working as a private chef for Dwayne Johnson. But apparently he's here now.

Holy buckets, Xavier, she thinks. *Good job.*

"Lizbet Keaton," Lizbet says, shaking his hand. "I'm the general manager of the hotel."

"Yes," he says. "I know."

"You're Mario *Subiaco!*" JJ sounds like a nine-year-old Pop Warner quarterback who's meeting Tom Brady. "You're a *legend,* man!"

Mario nods. "Thanks, that makes me feel really old. Who are you?"

"JJ O'Malley," he says. "I'm the chef/owner of the Deck."

Mario shrugs. "Never heard of it. But as a fellow chef, I'm going to ask you to let Lizbet here get to work." Mario checks with Lizbet. "If that's what you want?"

Suddenly, Lizbet is mortified that her messy personal life is on display in the parking lot like this, JJ with his serial-killer beard in his clogs, holding his phone (playing Dido), a dozen roses on the ground by his feet.

Lizbet smiles at JJ. "So good to see you again." Making a clean exit, she turns on her heel and follows Mario into the building. She hears the Dido song cut off. When she looks back, she catches a glimpse of JJ staring forlornly after her. *Revenge—check,* she thinks, and she feels a little sorry for him.

When Lizbet and Mario reach the service kitchen—which will be used for the complimentary continental breakfast and lunch by the pool—Lizbet says, "Thank you, but you didn't have to step in."

"I saw him grab you," Mario says. "I thought maybe you needed saving."

Immediately, Lizbet's starstruck awe diminishes. "I can take care of myself," Lizbet says. "And a lot of other people besides."

Mario has the gall to wink at her. "I'm guessing that was your ex-boyfriend, showing up to propose?"

It's none of Mario Subiaco's business who it was, but Lizbet doesn't need a feud between the hotel and the bar on the first day; there's plenty of time for that later.

"I should probably get upstairs," Lizbet says.

"I lied to him, you know," Mario says.

"Excuse me?"

"I told him I'd never heard of the Deck. I've been away from the island, sure, but I haven't been living on Mars. You two did some real stuff at that place, huh? A rosé fountain? Wish I'd thought of that seventeen years ago. And I heard the food was banging."

"'Those were the days, my friend, we thought they'd never end,'" Lizbet says. "Oh, but end they did. I left the Deck and I left him. We'll see what happens this summer."

Mario smirks. "This summer, I steal all his customers."

God, you're cocky, Lizbet thinks—or maybe in her caffeine mania she actually whispers it, because Mario bursts out laughing. "I know you need to be upstairs to start your very important general managing, but can I ask your quick opinion on something?" He waves her into the gleaming white-and-stainless-steel kitchen of the Blue Bar. Lizbet watches him for a second, thinking she'd like to put her stiletto right up his ass. It's only seven thirty in the morning and she's already had enough of chefs for one day.

But she follows him anyway.

"I was just back here doing a little mixology," Mario says. "Come see." He leads Lizbet over to a wide butcher block made of zebrawood—they spared no expense down here—that's crowded with fruit. There are tiny wild strawberries, kaffir limes, watermelons, blood oranges, kiwis, dragon fruits, rambutans, mangoes, two kinds of cherries (bing and golden Rainier), guavas, blackberries, coconuts, grapefruits, and something that looks like—yes, it is—a pink pineapple. It's a fruit festival, a fruit jamboree, a fruit *rave*. Down the counter is the alcohol, all top-shelf: Plymouth gin, Finlandia vodka, Casa Dragones tequila. Lizbet is impressed from a cost standpoint alone.

"I just need one more cocktail for my list. What do you think of this?" Mario reaches for a beaker filled with a liquid the color of a deep red sunset. He pours it into a stemless wineglass and tops it with champagne. It's Dom Pérignon, Lizbet realizes. Mario is doing his mixology experiments with *Dom*. That's quite a flex.

She shouldn't drink before eight a.m. on her first day of work, but Lizbet's focus is stretched out like a Slinky and she needs something to combat the aggressiveness of the espresso.

She takes a sip. *Gah!* So good. Another sip, in the interest of figuring out what's in the drink. Vodka. Strawberries. Ginger? Yes, there's a knob of ginger on the board. And some of the blood-orange juice.

She shrugs. "It's fine, I guess."

A slow smile crosses Mario's face and Lizbet takes a close look at him. In the magazine picture that hangs on JJ's office wall, Mario is much younger: smooth olive skin, thick dark hair, and a *Let me take you to bed* look in his eyes. He's older now; his hair and goatee are flecked with silver. He has lines cut deep into his forehead and radiating from the corners of his eyes. But he still has the swagger—and he knows this cocktail is the best thing Lizbet has ever tasted, that she would swim in it if she could.

"Well, then," he says. "We'll name that one for you. The Heartbreaker."

Magda English might be middle-aged, but her nephew Zeke has taught her some things. She knows that the rapper Pop Smoke is dead and that Wednesdays are called "Woo Back Wednesdays" in his honor. She knows about Polo G, House of Highlights, the Shade Room, and all things Barstool. She knows the modern meanings of *bet, sneaky link, bop, dip, bussin',* and *full send.* And Magda knows what a Chad is—it's a young man who embodies a certain stereotype of wealth and privilege: boarding school, college, trust fund, pastel polo shirts worn with the collar flipped up, golf, ski house, summer house, "vodka soda close it," and a river of money flowing from his adoring parents.

Therefore, Magda finds it amusing that the young man she's about to interview is actually named Chad. *Chadwick Winslow of Radnor, Pennsylvania,* the résumé on fine ivory stock announces. His appearance doesn't disappoint: He has shown up to the housekeeping office in khakis, pink shirt, a tie printed with starfish holding martinis, and a navy blazer. Boat shoes without socks. He has thick blond hair and the smooth cheeks of a child. His résumé also tells Magda that he's twenty-two, graduated from Bucknell with a major in "general humanities," and was in the Sigma Phi Epsilon fraternity. His previous work experience was as a counselor at a golf camp.

Although Magda has no idea what this child is doing in her office, she's not unhappy to see him. One of her four staff cleaners called to back out *yesterday,* the day before the hotel opened. When Magda informed Lizbet of this, Lizbet pulled young Master Winslow's résumé out of a folder that she jokingly (or maybe not) called "the Last Resort file."

"This kid stopped by the other day, insisting he wanted to clean. Honestly, I thought it was a prank. But feel free to call him and see if he was serious."

When Magda called, Chad sounded eager to come for an interview, and he showed up on time today—first hurdle cleared. But it could still be a prank, a bet, a dare, or a simple misunderstanding.

Magda says, "You realize, son, that I'm looking for *cleaning staff?*"

"Yes, ma'am."

"You're twenty-two, a college graduate. I could see you wanting to work the bell stand. But I don't understand why you'd want to clean hotel rooms."

Chad clears his throat. "I messed up. Badly."

"You won't get rich cleaning rooms," Magda says. "Have you asked about a job at the Blue Bar?"

"I want to clean rooms, ma'am."

But why? Magda thinks. *This makes no sense.* "Do you have any cleaning experience?" she asks.

"I help my mom around the house from time to time. And I was the social chair for my fraternity, so I was in charge of setting up for parties and cleaning up afterward."

Magda shakes her head, perplexed; she thought for sure he'd applied for the wrong job. From the looks of his clothes, he has plenty of money. And yet, she can see the earnestness on his face; for some reason, he wants *this* job. She studies the résumé. The local address he gave is Eel Point Road, which Magda has recently learned is high-roller real estate.

"Did your parents make you apply for this job? Are they trying to teach you some kind of lesson?"

"No, ma'am, it was my idea."

Young Chadwick Winslow sounds like he's telling the truth. Magda is intrigued.

"You would be the fourth and final member of our cleaning team, and as...the lacrosse coach at the Episcopal School might have informed you, there is no *I* in *team*. You won't get special treatment because you're male or because you have a college degree, and there will be no exceptions made because you went to the Chicken Box and are feeling too hungover to clean toilets. I need you here on time and ready to work. This isn't golf camp, Chadwick. It's stripping sheets and picking up wet towels and scrubbing shower stalls until they gleam. It's dealing with other people's excrement and urine and vomit and blood and semen and hair. I hope you have a strong stomach."

"I do."

Well, let's hope so, Magda thinks, *because I need someone today.* "I'm going to gamble and offer you the job," she says. She can't believe she's doing this. There's a 99 percent chance the kid won't last two weeks. He might not even last two days.

But Magda loves a long shot.

"Thank you," Chad says. "I won't let you down."

"You'll start right now," Magda says. "It's opening day, the rooms are all clean, and that will give me a chance to train you."

"Now is great!" Chad says. He has at least enough sense to take his blazer off and roll up his sleeves.

"So what did you do?" she asks. "When you messed up?"

"If you don't mind, I'd rather not say."

"It's none of my business," Magda says. "I was just curious. I happen to believe, Chadwick, that even the biggest disasters can be cleaned up, and I'll teach you to believe it too."

Edie Robbins wakes up on the morning of her first day of work on the front desk, checks her phone, and sees the e-mail from Xavier Darling. *Yes!* she thinks. *Yes-yes-yes!* Xavier is offering a thousand-dollar bonus per *week!* And it isn't a participation trophy! The same employee might win all eighteen weeks of the season!

Edie smells bacon frying. Just like every year on Edie's first day of school, there will be bacon and eggs for breakfast and Tater Tot Hotdish for dinner. Edie's mother, Love, is trying to keep everything in their lives the same—even though nothing has been the same since Edie's father, Vance Robbins, died of a heart attack. Although Love says she's "doing okay"—she has taken a full-time job at Flowers on Chestnut to "keep busy"—Edie can sense she's still grieving. This is why Edie decided to spend the summer at home. Also, she had to get away from her ex-boyfriend Graydon.

Edie's plan is to save as much money as she can over the summer and apply for a job out in the "real world"—New York, São Paulo, London, Sydney, Shanghai—in the fall. She has a crippling student-loan payment (the Ivy League wasn't cheap), so although her hourly pay is more than she anticipated, an extra thousand dollars would really help.

She will win it, she decides. She'll win it every week. She is ready to slay!

Edie's fiercest competition for the prize money will be her partner on the front desk, Alessandra Powell. When Edie arrives at work— nearly ten minutes early—Alessandra is already there, and she has nabbed the more desirable computer, the one closest to the open end of the desk (Edie will have to scoot by Alessandra every time she comes or goes).

"Good morning, Alessandra!" Edie says brightly.

Alessandra does an oh-so-quick-but-still-noticeable up-and-down of Edie, presses her lips together, and says in a tone that is not cold but also not warm, "Good morning."

Edie wills herself not to take offense; from what Edie observed at training and during the first staff meeting, Alessandra is stand-offish. (Maybe not a mean girl, but maybe not *not* a mean girl.) That, Edie can deal with. She has a harder time accepting that Alessandra is the front-desk manager. Edie doesn't understand why there has to be a front-desk manager when there are only two desk people hired so far. Edie realizes that Alessandra is older and has more practical job experience and speaks four languages. But something about Alessandra having the title feels wrong. She just walked in off the street; it's her first summer on Nantucket; Lizbet doesn't know her and neither does anyone else on this island.

The night before, at dinner, Edie complained about the situation to her mother. Love worked for years as the front-desk manager at the Nantucket Beach Club, and Edie's father, Vance, had been the night manager.

Love sipped her wine. "I bet the two of you will be best friends by the end of the summer."

"That's such a mom thing to say."

"Sorry," Love said. "I bet the two of you are going to have a tumultuous summer marked by incidents of envious backstabbing."

Envious, yes, Edie thinks now. Not only is Alessandra gorgeous and multilingual but she's a walking, talking Pinterest board. Edie and Alessandra are wearing the same uniform—white pants and a silky hydrangea-blue button-down blouse. Alessandra has accessorized her uniform with a Johnnie-O canvas color-block belt that probably belongs to her boyfriend (but looks *so cute!*), a pair of taupe wedge sandals, and a collection of gold bangles—among which is a Cartier love bracelet—that make bright jangly sounds every time Alessandra moves her left arm. Her reddish-blond hair is long, tousled, and beachy, yet not a strand is out of place (how is that possible?). She's wearing white eyeliner and has a tiny crystal pressed under her right eye. (At college, Edie thought eye crystals were trashy, but on Alessandra it looks chic. How is that possible?) Her name tag is upside down, which Edie thinks is a mistake but then realizes must be intentional—a conversation starter—because she can tell that Alessandra doesn't make mistakes.

Edie, by contrast, has her hair held back in a headband, no belt (she didn't think to wear a belt), and Skechers on her feet because she was worried about being comfortable. Her name tag is right side up.

"Thank you for setting up the coffee," Edie says as she logs onto the computer next to the wall. She tries not to feel hemmed in or trapped (she feels both). Alessandra's bracelets chatter in response and Edie thinks, *Fine, whatever.* The coffee smells rich and delicious and Edie wonders if she can pour herself a cup; Lizbet didn't say one way or the other.

But at that moment, Edie sees her mother's coworker Joan, from Flowers on Chestnut, rolling in a cart laden with the bouquets for the rooms. They have guests for eleven rooms checking in today and they've ordered a dozen Surfside Spring arrangements—enormous blue hydrangeas, pink starburst lilies, flame-orange snapdragons, and blush peonies curled up into tight little balls. Joan also has a supersize version of this arrangement for the pedestal table in the lobby.

"Sweet Edie!" Joan cries out. "Look at you on your *first day of work!* Your mom is so proud of you."

"Good morning, Joan," Edie says. She hears Alessandra murmur, "Sweet Edie?" and Edie feels herself flush. That's the thing about working on your home island, she thinks. Everyone knows you, and they all call you by your mortifying nickname. She has been Sweet Edie since she was small, her father's fault.

Edie moves the large arrangement to the lobby while Alessandra tasks the short, floppy-haired bellman named Adam with delivering eleven of the arrangements to the rooms. The twelfth arrangement goes back in Lizbet's office.

Joan reenters the lobby holding a planter of glorious deep purple vanda orchids.

"Those are stunning vandas," Edie says, showing off her orchid knowledge for Alessandra. "Are they for me?" She's kidding. That's at least four hundred dollars' worth of orchids, and although Edie's mother is proud of her, they don't have that kind of money to throw around.

"These are for Magda English," Joan says. "Seems she has an admirer."

Magda English! Edie thinks. That's Zeke English's aunt, the head of housekeeping.

"I'll take them to her." Edie carries the orchids down the hall to the housekeeping office, where she catches Magda just leaving with a blond guy about Edie's age who's wearing a pink oxford shirt and a needlepoint belt. He looks like one of the obnoxious summer kids who elbow other people out of the way to throw down their parents' credit cards at the Gazebo.

"Ms. English, these came for you," Edie says. "You have an admirer."

Magda stops in her tracks and stares at the flowers, then tsks and shakes her head. "Put them on my desk, please, dear," she says. "Chadwick and I have work to do."

Chadwick, Edie thinks, trying to hide her smile. *Chad!* She sets the orchids on Magda's desk and stares at the small envelope gripped in the prongs of the plastic stake. The envelope is sealed, and Edie can't very well open it, but she's tempted to hold it up to the sunlight streaming through the window so she can see who has sent Magda English these extravagant flowers.

Edie has successfully checked guests into two rooms and one suite when a family bursts into the lobby. It's a mother and two children, one girl, one boy. The mother is tall and supermodel-thin—she's all flat chest and protruding hip bones—and she has what Edie can only describe as "peacock hair," dyed ombré streaks of green and blue. She's either way cooler than your average mother, Edie thinks, or going through a midlife crisis.

Edie is on hold with Cru, attempting to secure a dinner reservation for the Katzens in room 103. She watches the little boy make a mad dash for one of the chess sets. When he picks up a knight and moves it, Edie hangs up.

"Louie!" the mother says. "Get back here this instant."

"They have chess!" Louie shouts. He goes to the opposite side of the board and moves a pawn.

Next to Edie, Alessandra snaps to attention and gives the family her radiant (and phony) smile. "Welcome—"

"Welcome to the Hotel Nantucket!" Edie calls out, stepping on Alessandra's words.

Without removing her sunglasses, the peacock-haired mother looks from Edie to Alessandra as though she's arrived at a fork in the road. She seems inclined to go to Alessandra, and Edie wonders if she will be forced to suffer this rejection check-in after check-in, day after day, all summer long. Given the choice between Edie and Alessandra, people will always choose Alessandra, either because she's beautiful or because she radiates the mesmerizing self-confidence of a Kardashian.

Edie waves the woman over so there can be no mistake. "I'll check you in!"

Alessandra's bracelets clinkety-clank. It's the passive-aggressive sound of her discontent. Thankfully, the phone rings and Alessandra answers it. Edie splinters her attention long enough to realize that it's the hostess from Cru calling back. Alessandra can handle the Katzens' dinner reservation.

"Okay?" the peacock-haired woman says. She approaches with her children now firmly in hand. Both have white-blond hair and are wearing little round spectacles with thick lenses that make their eyes look like pale blue fish swimming behind glass; they're so odd-looking, they're cute. "My name is Kimber Marsh and this is Wanda and Louie. We'd like to book a room."

"I can certainly help you with that," Edie says. Their first walk-in! Lizbet will be thrilled; she confided to Edie that she's concerned about their low occupancy. "What kind of room would best suit your needs?"

"I'd say we need a room with two queens. I can't very well get them their own room, they're too young."

"For how many nights?"

"I'd like to stay for the entire summer."

The entire summer? Edie thinks. She starts vibrating with excitement. This is what Lizbet has been hoping for: people hearing about the hotel and walking in off the street to book rooms.

"The rate on our deluxe guest room with two queen beds is three twenty-five," Edie says. "With tax and fees, that room is four hundred dollars."

"That's fine," Kimber says. "Please book us until..." She pulls up the calendar on her phone. "The kids have to be back in school then...add a few days to get ready...let's say August twenty-fifth."

Edie checks her availability, glances at Alessandra, who is just hanging up with Cru, and says, "Tell you what, I'm going to give you a free upgrade to one of our family suites." The hotel has twelve suites and only one of them has been booked, so Edie feels fine about upgrading Kimber Marsh. The suites are divine and, in Edie's opinion, should not be left languishing. Suite 114, which is the one Edie is giving the Marsh family, has a big living area with a full wall of brand-new hardcover books, all for the guests' reading pleasure, and there's a window seat overlooking Easton Street. This particular suite has a master bedroom and a whimsical room for kids with four wide bunk beds connected by tunnels and rope bridges; there are hidden reading nooks, and there's even a swing. It's very extra. Wanda and Louie will love it.

"You're upgrading us?" Kimber says. She raises her sunglasses to the top of her head so she can read Edie's name tag. "Edie Robbins, you're an angel fallen to earth."

Edie studies Kimber's face. She has bleary-looking blue eyes with brownish-purple rings beneath them; she reminds Edie of a beleaguered mom in a laundry-detergent commercial. Edie fills with joy at being able to offer this nice blue-and-green-haired woman an upgrade. "It's my enormous and whole-hearted pleasure," she says. She's overcome with a sense of professional pride and fulfillment.

This is what hospitality is about—offering the guests something extra, something that makes them feel special, singled out and tended to. "I'll just need to run a credit card."

"Well, that's the thing," Kimber says. She glances at the children, who are as still as sentinels beside her. "Kids, go play chess, please. But only *one* game."

"I don't want to play chess," Wanda says. "I want to read." She holds up a book that Edie recognizes—a vintage Nancy Drew mystery with the canary-yellow back cover. *The Secret of Shadow Ranch*. Edie read the same edition when she was Wanda's age.

"Please, Wanda?" Louie says. "I'll let you win."

Edie laughs and Kimber rolls her eyes. "He's *obsessed.* He brought a travel chess set with him, of course, but he accidentally left it at the Connecticut welcome center and it was a river of tears all the way up I-95. I hope you like children, because we'll never get him out of here. He'll sit at that chessboard all summer."

Edie laughs again, though a little less enthusiastically. Louie is able to drag Wanda over to the chessboard while Edie waits to hear what "thing" Kimber is talking about.

When the children are out of earshot, Kimber says, "I was hoping I could pay cash."

"Cash?" Edie says. The woman is booking a room for four hundred dollars a night for eighty-one nights and she wants to pay *cash?*

Kimber drops her voice to a whisper. "I'm in the midst of a divorce, so both of my cards have been frozen because they draw on joint accounts, yada-yada. I have cash, but I won't be able to give you a card, I'm afraid."

Edie blinks. Who in the year 2022 is crazy enough to think she could check into a luxury hotel without a credit card?

"The charge won't go through," Edie says. "We just put a minimum hold on it, fifty dollars per night."

Kimber Marsh says, "What I'm telling you is that it's not going to work, the card will be declined." She clears her throat. "We tried this already at the Faraway."

"Ah," Edie says. The Faraway is a fairly new boutique hotel in the center of town. If the Faraway didn't let Kimber Marsh check in without a credit card, then Edie obviously shouldn't either. But...she knows it's the hotel's mission to *distinguish* itself from the other luxury hotels on the island. Why shouldn't they accept cash? Cash is money. But then Edie recalls the unspoken-but-understood reality of the hotel business: Guests lie. Their relationship with you—meaning the hotel staff—is temporary, so they feel they can say whatever they want. How many case studies did Edie read at Cornell about handling sticky situations with guests? Dozens— and yet none exactly like this. Her ex-boyfriend Graydon would probably say that Kimber Marsh was trying to pull a con, using her children as a smoke screen. She *says* she has cash, but what if she doesn't? And even if she does, is she just going to hand over a stack of bills?

Edie needs to speak to Lizbet.

"I'll just be one second," Edie says. She pops into the back office and calls Lizbet's cell, but it goes straight to voice mail. Ugh. She remembers that Lizbet is giving a tour of the property to the couple from Syracuse checking into room 303 and shouldn't be interrupted. Every guest is a potential influencer.

Alessandra comes back into the office. "You're letting those guests *wither*."

Wither, really? Edie thinks. She's been gone less than sixty seconds. "I need to speak to Lizbet."

"Why don't you let me take over their check-in since you're not comfortable doing it."

"I'm comfortable," Edie says. She brushes past Alessandra, goes back out to the desk where Kimber Marsh waits. Edie hears Louie say, "Checkmate." He starts setting the board up again while Wanda sinks back into the armchair and opens her book. "I really need to speak to my GM before I okay this," Edie says.

Kimber Marsh leans in. "My soon-to-be-ex-husband left me for my nanny." She emits a short, bitter laugh. "It's such a cliché, but the reality is, I lost my spouse *and* my help. Craig and Jenny are spending the summer together in the Hamptons—Jenny just found out she's *pregnant*—so I wanted to take my kids away rather than let them stew in the cauldron that is New York City. But not having a functioning credit card *is* an issue, I realize this." She pauses. "What if I give you the first week in cash with an extra five hundred dollars thrown on top for incidentals?" She sighs. "Can you work with me? Please?"

Left her for the nanny? Edie thinks. *Who's pregnant?* Of course Edie can work with her. This poor woman needs her help. Kimber Marsh wants her kids to have a fun summer, and Edie is going to make that happen (and maybe win the thousand-dollar bonus for her superlative service!).

She hears Alessandra's bracelets but she doesn't look over. She slides two key cards across the desk. "I'll discuss your payment options with my GM, but for now, let's get you settled in your suite."

Alessandra clears her throat.

"Do you have luggage?" Edie asks.

"Yes, the gentlemen out front…" Kimber checks behind her. "There's quite a lot of stuff. I think they're just unpacking the car."

"And they have Doug!" Wanda reappears, though Louie has made himself comfortable over at the chessboard.

"Excellent," Edie says. She has no idea who Doug is; maybe a stuffed animal, maybe an imaginary friend. "I can't wait to meet him. Since the bellmen are busy with your luggage, I'll show you the way." At this point, Edie has no choice but to turn to

Alessandra. "I'm just showing the Marsh family to their suite, I'll be back in a moment."

Alessandra's smile is glacial. "Of course." And then to Kimber: "Enjoy your stay and let us know if there's anything we can do for you."

No sooner does Edie emerge from behind the desk than Adam walks in with the luggage trolley, filled to the tippy-top with bags. Adam catches Edie's eye and says something under his breath that Edie doesn't hear and, based on his tone and facial expression, probably doesn't want to hear. A second later, Zeke English, who graduated from Nantucket High School two years ahead of Edie and who is so smoking hot he makes Edie feel kind of dizzy, comes into the lobby with a dog on a leash—a lean and muscled blue-brindled pit bull. Edie knows the breed because Graydon, her ex, had a pit bull named Portia. This dog, who is wearing a black muzzle, pulls Zeke along, its nails skating across the rare wormy chestnut floors of the lobby.

Edie's mouth drops open and she looks at Zeke and then Adam—but it's clear they're both expecting her to handle this. "Is this Doug?" Edie chirps.

Kimber's expression brightens. "Yes. I put the muzzle on him in the minivan, which he was *not* happy about. He's a sweet couch hippo, but he can act up around strangers."

He can act up around strangers, so why not bring him to a resort where there will be strangers around constantly? Edie starts to sweat. When you want to spend the summer on Nantucket with your children and your dog, you rent a house. Why didn't Kimber Marsh rent a house? It's possible she couldn't find a suitable rental at the last minute. Or maybe she didn't want the upkeep. Maybe she wanted a pool, a wellness center, and room service. There could be lots of reasons, but one thing has become clear: Edie needs to speak to Lizbet. She's too anxious to gauge Alessandra's reaction.

"Will you take Ms. Marsh and the children to their suite?" Edie says to Adam. "I'm going to call Lizbet."

"What about the dog?" Zeke asks. "Take him?"

All Edie can picture is Doug jumping up on the sumptuous white bed, chewing on the rope and driftwood frame, clawing at the white sheers, peeing on the Annie Selke rug. She gets the shivers. She figures the Faraway turned the Marshes down not because of the cash but because of the dog. "Would you and Doug wait outside for two seconds until I speak to Lizbet?"

Zeke looks put out; the dog quite obviously wants to follow the rest of the family but Zeke shepherds him back outside. Edie glances at Alessandra, who offers ice-cap eyes. She's not going to help. Okay, fine. Edie pops into the back office and tries Lizbet again, and this time Lizbet answers.

"Lizbet?" Edie says. "We've had our first walk-ins! It's a woman named Kimber Marsh and her two children. They want to stay for the entire summer and they're paying cash."

"Please tell me you got a credit card, Edie," Lizbet says.

"She's going through a divorce, so both her cards are frozen. She said she'll give us the first week plus five hundred for incidentals—"

"Oh no, Edie!"

Only now does Edie realize how absurd this sounds, and she's barely started. "I upgraded her to suite one fourteen because it was empty."

"You upgraded her," Lizbet says. "For the entire summer? Please tell me you're joking."

"Those family suites are just sitting vacant."

"They'll fill up," Lizbet says. "And when they do, we'll lose room revenue on your eleven-week upgrade."

Edie has messed this whole thing up. If this were role-playing back in college, she would get nothing but "feedback for improvement."

Here in the real world, she might get fired, and she hasn't even told Lizbet the worst part.

"Also," Edie says, "she has a pit bull. His name is Doug."

"What?" Lizbet says.

Edie kisses her dream of this week's thousand-dollar bonus goodbye.

6. Staff Secrets

In her century as a ghost, Grace has developed and honed her EQ; her instincts about people are (nearly) always correct. Grace can sense trouble—it feels as though she's hearing a wrong note in a song or tasting a wine that has gone off. And while Grace is intrigued by the unexpected arrival of this family, she sees a flashing yellow light of warning when she looks at the mother. Kimber Marsh is lying about something. The children, however, are precious little angels, so cute and odd that Grace would like to cuddle them.

The children run, shouting, into the bunk-room wonderland of suite 114 with the dog following at a trot. The little boy, Louie, scales the ladder to the top bunk closest to the door, then clambers across a rope bridge to the other top bunk. The little girl, Wanda, tucks herself into the swing that looks like a wicker egg and opens her mystery book. Doug the dog stops just inside the threshold of the room and raises his bucket head. He starts to whine.

Oh, snap, Grace thinks. He senses her; animals nearly always do.

"What's wrong, Dougie?" Wanda says. "Come on."

Grace floats into the master bedroom, where Kimber Marsh runs a finger along the spines of the books lining the shelves. She's really quite lovely when she smiles, Grace thinks, though the green and blue hair is unsettling. And something else is off.

Kimber opens the small icebox and pulls out a package of crackers, a tub of smoked bluefish pâté, and—well, it is five o'clock in Greenland—a bottle of cranberry pinot gris from Nantucket Vineyards. She pours the glass of sparkling wine, then drags the cracker through the pâté and shoves it into her mouth. Grace forgives her table manners because she's so thin and needs to eat. Then Kimber slips over to the tablet by the bedside and suddenly the room fills with music. It's Mötley Crüe singing "Home Sweet Home." Grace hasn't heard this song since the early nineties.

Kimber goes into the bathroom with her toiletries and Grace follows cautiously; she has to avoid the mirrors just in case Kimber has, as it was popular to say in the late nineties, "a sixth sense." (*I see dead people.*) Kimber glances around, sniffs the Nest candle by the tub (Amalfi lemon and mint), turns on the soft halo light around the mirror, and winks at her reflection. *Okay?* Grace thinks. *Let's unpack this: Why would a person wink at herself? She's pulled something off? She doesn't have a penny to her name but now she and the children and the dog are ensconced in these glorious digs?*

Back in the bedroom, Kimber has another cracker and then, from the mess of luggage they brought, she fishes out a red duffel. She unzips it to reveal thick bricks of cash. *So she wasn't bluffing about the money,* Grace thinks. As she's stacking the cash in the safe in the walk-in closet, there's a knock at the door. Kimber tenses, then creeps out to the living room. She looks through the peephole and smiles.

It's Grace's crush Zeke (*sigh*) holding one of the marble chess sets from the lobby. "Edie said that Louie lost his travel chess set. She thought he might like to have a board of his own for the room."

"Thank you!" Kimber said. "How thoughtful." She holds up a finger. "Let me get you a little something."

"No need," Zeke says. "It's our pleasure."

Lizbet has just finished showing the couple from Syracuse around—the woman said she had a "nice" following on Instagram, and Lizbet thought she might help spread the word about the hotel—and she's been on her feet all day long (what possessed her to wear stilettos?), but when Edie tells her about the family in suite 114, she hustles back to the office. All she can think as she collapses into her chair is that Sweet Edie was duped on day one by some grifter.

She has to go to suite 114.

Lizbet limps down the hall and knocks on the door with a smile on her face that's so forced, it makes her head ache.

Kimber Marsh opens the door. Thank God Edie warned Lizbet about the hair, because it's startling. "Ms. Marsh, hello. I'm Lizbet Keaton, the general manager of the hotel."

"What a beautiful property you have here," she says. "The kids are in heaven."

Lizbet had meant to be firm but when the two little towheaded children in glasses tiptoe out of the bunk room, she relents immediately. The girl is holding a book, and the boy clutches a white chess queen. "I spoke with Edie, who checked you in. She told me you'd like to pay in cash, which is fine. I'll need the first week as a deposit."

"Yes, of course. One second." Kimber heads into the bedroom and reappears a moment later with a stack of bills. She counts it out: thirty-three hundred dollars. "The first week plus five hundred for incidentals. I can pay in advance every Monday if that's easiest?"

"In advance every Monday works," Lizbet says, relaxing a bit. If the woman pays in advance, there's no problem, is there? "We'll slip an invoice under the door and e-mail it to you as well."

Kimber Marsh opens her arms and hugs Lizbet, and the children run over and grab Lizbet around the legs. Over Kimber's shoulder, Lizbet sees the dog. He trots over to sniff Lizbet, then plops down at her aching feet.

At the end of the day, Lizbet calls the staff to her office. Raoul, who is working night bell, agrees to watch the desk.

Lizbet gathers Edie, Alessandra, Zeke, Adam, and Magda, who is trailed by a preppy-looking kid wearing rumpled khakis and a pink oxford shirt rolled up above his elbows.

"Lizbet, let me introduce the newest member of my housekeeping staff, Chadwick Winslow," Magda says. "I trained him today. The other cleaners won't be in until the morning."

"Chad Winslow," the kid says, shaking Lizbet's hand.

"That's right, I remember when you dropped off your résumé. I'm glad this worked out. Welcome."

Chad dips his head. "Thank you for the chance. I'm grateful."

Chadwick Winslow sounds like a name straight off the *Mayflower* manifest, but Lizbet wants to foster diversity and inclusivity across the board. Why shouldn't a rich-looking dude named Chad be cleaning rooms?

Lizbet leads everyone into the break room, which has been decorated to resemble a 1950s diner; there's the signature turquoise and orange of a Howard Johnson's and a lot of chrome and Formica. It provides a complete psychological separation from the rest of the hotel, which is important when everyone is working six and a half days a week. There's a bar counter where the staff can sit and eat lunch, a low, curvy sofa with plenty of pillows for napping, a soft-serve ice cream machine, a vintage pinball machine—Hokus Pokus—and a jukebox that gives four plays for a dollar. Lizbet is seriously impressed by the break room, but for the most part, the staff seem nonplussed. Zeke stares at the pinball machine like it's a Martian spacecraft, and Lizbet can see him wishing there was a TV and a PS5 instead. Edie inspects the songs on the jukebox and says, "I've never heard of any of this music. Who's Joan Jett?"

Lizbet asks everyone to sit and then checks that the door is closed tight.

"First of all, I want to thank you all for your great work today." She brings her hands together in front of her chest. The incident with JJ and Mario Subiaco that morning in the parking lot feels like three days ago, and Lizbet has to stay to work the night desk. How is she ever going to make it through the summer?

She isn't, at this rate, and especially not in heels.

"We have guests in suite one fourteen who will be staying for the summer. I just want to remind everyone that although these guests may become very familiar to you over time, you should always treat them with the highest standards of service. And information about all our guests should be held in the strictest confidence."

"Of course," Edie says. Everyone else just nods.

Something about Kimber Marsh's cash felt fishy, and after the children and Doug retreated back to their room, Lizbet had wanted to ask Kimber a question—but she wasn't sure what that question should be. Was her ex-husband abusive? Was he in the Mob or a drug dealer? Was the family in hiding? In the end, Lizbet said to Kimber, "We're so glad you're here. I wrote a Nantucket recommendation guide, which I'm calling the Blue Book. I'll leave it for you at the desk." Then Lizbet zipped down to her computer and googled Kimber Marsh of East Seventy-Fourth Street, New York, New York. Nothing relevant came up. Lizbet checked Facebook, Twitter, and Instagram—nothing. She tried Kimberly Marsh, Kim Marsh, Kimmy Marsh—still nothing. As far as the internet was concerned, Kimber Marsh didn't exist. Was that suspicious? Lizbet reasoned that there were lots of people who didn't use social media. Or maybe because of the divorce, she had deleted her accounts.

To the staff, Lizbet says, "I've advised Ms. Marsh to use the exit next to her suite to walk the dog. The last thing I want to see is that dog strolling through the lobby."

"I'll walk the dog for Ms. Marsh if she needs me," Zeke says.

Edie laughs. "Seriously? This afternoon, that dog was walking you."

"We bonded," Zeke says. "It'll be my pleasure to do that for Ms. Marsh."

"He just wants the thousand-dollar bonus," Adam says.

"About those bonuses," Lizbet says, and every pair of eyes snaps back to her. "In addition to reading the TravelTattler reviews, Mr. Darling will be hearing from *me* about staff performance. And what I'll be looking for is superlative guest service, of course, but also selflessness, sacrifice, promptness, consistency, kindness, and teamwork."

Alessandra, who has been sitting on the sofa with her arms crossed, raises a hand. "Will Mr. Darling be in residence this summer?"

"Not until August."

Alessandra frowns, but the rest of the staff look relieved. Adam raises his hand. "Can we get the piano in the lobby tuned?" he asks.

"Sure," Lizbet says. Until this second, she thought of the piano only as a piece of furniture. "Do you play?"

"I do," Adam says. He sings out "Welcome to the Hotel Na-antucket!" to the tune of "Hotel California," and everyone except Alessandra smiles. He has a great voice, a Broadway voice—just like his former GM said in the e-mail.

"I'll put that on my list," Lizbet says. She looks around the room. "Does anyone else have hidden talents?" She pauses. "Or perhaps a secret to share in this safe space?"

She watches every face in the room tense up.

Lizbet smiles. "Just kidding, guys. Thank you for a terrific first day."

Lizbet *isn't* kidding. She wants to nurture intimacy and trust. During her fifteen seasons at the Deck, Lizbet was a vault for all sorts of sensitive information. She was the first call when Goose's brother got arrested for a DUI; she sat with Juliette in the restaurant office while Juliette cried about accidentally getting pregnant. However, Lizbet kept boundaries in place—she was 90 percent boss, 10 percent big sister. Her staffers were a little afraid of her, but that meant she was doing a good job. She wants to create that same atmosphere here; it's her *strength*. She scrutinizes her staff. If they're hiding anything—as she suspects Kimber Marsh is—she wants to know about it now.

Chad Winslow leaves the staff meeting and drives his brand-new Range Rover back to his parents' summer house on Eel Point Road.

Secrets? he thinks. There's no way Lizbet could have heard what happened back in Pennsylvania, but the question made him uncomfortable.

He checks his phone only long enough to see that it's clogged with texts and snaps from his summer friends, but there's nothing from Paddy, which is both agonizing and a relief. Chad has texted Paddy every day since he arrived on the island but he's heard nothing back. Paddy is finished with Chad, hates his guts, will never speak to him again. And the thing is, Chad can't blame him. As Chad rumbles down the dirt road past the grandest beachfront homes on the island, he recalls Ms. English's words: *I happen to believe, Chadwick, that even the biggest disasters can be cleaned up, and I'll teach you to believe it too.* Chad wants to believe it. He wants to think that if he works hard and keeps his eyes straight ahead, he'll be able to scour the ugly stain from his life.

Ms. English and Chad spent all day in room 104, which was already impeccably clean. She stripped the sheets off the emperor-size bed and he started from scratch, pulling the fitted sheet tight around the corners. *Nothing worse than a rumpled bottom sheet,* Ms. English said. She showed him how to arrange the pillows; she made him take a picture of the finished product as though it were an art installation. They spent two hours in the bathroom alone, going over all the places on a toilet where bacteria hides, how to find and dispose of stray hairs and clipped nails, how to get water stains off the drinking glasses, and how to fold a towel, which was harder than it looked; Chad folded the same towel sixty-two times, starting over if the edges weren't straight. They ran through the one hundred points on the checklist, including the tiniest details that Chad never would have thought about—the number of hangers in the closets, whether all the light bulbs worked, and the temperature of the minifridge. Ms. English gave Chad strict instructions about which of the guests' belongings it was okay to touch; he was to fold discarded clothes and place them on the surface closest to where he found them. (The guests will always leave their underwear draped over the telephone, Ms. English told him, which made him laugh. He hoped she was kidding.) He was never to touch jewelry, watches, or cash unless it was a checkout and the cash had been left as a tip. He was never to go into the drawers, the closet, or a suitcase.

Obviously, Chad said, and Ms. English had given him a pointed look. Did she think he was a thief? He hadn't told her how he'd "messed up," so it was possible she thought he'd stolen something.

That was practically the only thing he hadn't done.

When Chad pulls into his driveway, he sees his friend Jasper's Porsche Cayenne parked there, and Jasper, Bryce, and Eric are standing on the front porch.

Chad aims the air-conditioning vents straight at his face and wishes he could disappear.

"Where you been, bruh, snapping you all day, we finally decided to storm the castle but your sister said you weren't home, and when we asked her where you were, she said she hoped you were bleeding in a ditch."

"Ouch," Chad says, though this comes as no surprise. Leith hates him now.

"She's cold," Bryce says.

"And yet so hot," Eric says.

Chad doesn't have the energy to flip Eric off for that. He's more concerned about the sweet green miasma hanging in the air above his friends.

"You guys smoked up on my porch?"

"We were *waiting* for you, man. We're hitting the brewery. You have to come."

"I can't."

"Whaaaaa?" Eric says. "Band is back together, bruh, come on. Didn't you miss us?"

The answer is no. Chad is still friends with these guys—the young princes of Greenwich, Connecticut; Mission Hills, Kansas; and Fisher Island, Florida—only because of their shared past. They threw sand at one another on Children's Beach, sneaked into R-rated movies at the Dreamland Theater, showed up late to steak night at the Sankaty Head Golf Club with their oxfords half untucked and their eyes bloodshot because they'd smoked out of an apple pipe at Altar Rock. But thanks to his friendship with Paddy, Chad has gained a modicum of self-awareness. He realizes that the Chad stereotype—passing out in public (like Jasper in front of the Gazebo on Figawi weekend) or stranding a car on the beach (like Eric in his father's Mercedes at Fisherman's)—is not only privileged and elitist but also ridiculous and pathetic.

What do you call a group of Chads? An inheritance.

However, this self-awareness, of which Chad is secretly proud, was tragically lacking on May 22.

Chad is amazed these guys haven't heard what happened back in Radnor; he half expected his sister, Leith, to spill the beans, even though their parents swore both children to silence "for the sake of the family name." Still, Chad knows that gossip flows fast along tributaries slicked by money and privilege. How did news of the party not reach these three?

Or maybe it did, and they just don't care.

The brewery sounds like fun. They can have a couple of cold Whale's Tales, get some lobster sliders from the food trucks, check out girls, listen to live music, pet other people's golden retrievers. (*No,* Chad thinks, *no dogs.*)

He'll go for an hour, he thinks, to appease them.

But then he recalls how an hour or two at the brewery can easily turn into drinks at the Gazebo, which will then become the four of them lined up in the front row of the Chicken Box, pumping their fists in the air to some cover band singing Coldplay before spilling out onto Dave Street and puking out the back of a cab.

Chad needs to be at work bright and early tomorrow. He will *not* show up hungover.

"Good seeing you guys," Chad says.

"Man, what's going on?" Bryce says. "You didn't open a single snap all day and now you won't go out with us?"

Chad knows his behavior must seem strange. He's never been the ringleader of this group—that has always been Jasper—but in summers past, he's gone along for a good time.

"Where were you all day?" Jasper asks.

"I..." Chad says. He could tell these guys he got a job, but there would be follow-up questions like "Where?" and "Why?" Chad is supposed to be having one last summer of carefree leisure before starting at his father's venture-capital firm, the Brandywine Group, in September. How can Chad explain that not only is he working this summer, he's a *chambermaid?* He spent today in rubber gloves, learning about disinfectants. "Maybe I'll meet you guys later." He reaches for the doorknob so there can be no mistake: he's not going anywhere with them.

Eric cracks a big, high smile. "Chad must have himself a lady friend. Look at his 'fit—did he even come *home* last night?"

Jasper and Bryce start catcalling—"Bros before hos, man, but no worries, we're gonna dip"; "We'll hit you up later"—as Chad slips into the cool air of the foyer and closes the door behind him. Leith is coming down the stairs; she flips him off and heads for the kitchen without a word. His sister has recently earned her doctorate in the silent treatment, which hurts because they used to be friends.

A second later, he hears his mother, Whitney. "Chaddy?"

If she's calling him the world's worst nickname—Chaddy—then she's already into the chardonnay. Chad pokes his head into the kitchen and sees Whitney standing at the island with a large, uncorked bottle of Kendall-Jackson in front of her.

She flutters a piece of paper in his direction. "Pretty please," she says. "Market for Mom?"

He takes the list: *8 wagyu steaks, 3 lbs. bluefin tuna, 2 lbs. lobster salad, Comté cheese, truffled potato chips (6 bags).*

"This is a lot of food," he says. "Are we having company?"

Whitney shrugs and casts her eyes down into the golden promise of her wine. "Things for dinner."

Chad's father won't arrive on the island for another few weeks; he's busy closing a deal. Leith consumes only two things—hard-boiled eggs and Diet Dr Pepper—and Whitney eats even less than that. Yet his mother always stocks the fridge like the offensive line of the Philadelphia Eagles are coming for dinner. When she goes to the trouble of cooking, 90 percent of the food is pitched straight into the trash (neither of Chad's parents believes in leftovers). But most of the time, Whitney can't be bothered to cook. Instead, she pours wine, microwaves a bag of popcorn, and gets lost in Netflix or she meets "the girls" at the yacht club, and the groceries sit in the fridge until they grow a slimy film or greenish-gray fur. This never bothered Chad; he never even *noticed* until Paddy went on a tirade about the "conspicuous waste" of the Winslow household.

He'll buy three steaks, the cheese, and one bag of potato chips, he decides.

"I got a job today," he says.

"You did not." These are the first words Leith has spoken to him since May 22.

"At the Hotel Nantucket," Chad says. "Cleaning rooms."

His mother blinks.

"I wanted to do something," Chad says. "To make things right."

"Your father is handling it with the lawyers," his mother says.

"*I* wanted to do something. Get an honest job, make my own money to give to Paddy."

"Oh, sweetheart," Whitney says.

"Wait," Leith says. "You're serious? You're going to clean rooms at the hotel? You're going to be a…a…"

"Maid," Chad says. He watches his sister smile, which is nice because she has such a pretty smile and he hasn't seen it in a while. But then she dissolves into hysterical laughter that quickly becomes more hysteria than laughter and finishes as ugly sobs. She takes the closest thing she can find—a coffee mug with a picture of a dachshund on it—and throws it at him, hurling it like she's trying to get a lacrosse ball into the net for the game-winning goal against a longtime rival. She misses Chad; the mug smashes against the tile floor.

"You! Can't! Make! Things! Right!" she screams.

Chad leaves the kitchen and heads out the front door with the list clenched in his fist.

His sister is correct—he can't make things right. But he's going to die trying.

Since arriving on Nantucket last August and moving into the guest cottage behind her brother's house on West Chester Street, Magda English has established a tidy and modest routine. She attends the seven-thirty service at the Summer Street church every Sunday morning; she occasionally meets the church ladies (led by the sanctimonious and nearly unbearable Nancy Twine) for afternoons of "crafting"; and she cooks—soups, stews, and rice dishes, all of them diabolically spicy.

When Magda leaves the staff meeting, she chuckles to herself. *Does anyone have a secret to share in this safe space?*

Magda has secrets but she isn't fool enough to divulge them to people she's just met, most of whom aren't old enough to remember the turn of the millennium. She finds it amusing that their new general manager, a woman well into her thirties, is naive enough to believe that any space is "safe."

If Magda were going to lead by example and share something, it might have been this: She's thrilled to be working again. Her tidy and modest routine had grown dull; she was bored and more than once she had checked flights back to St. Thomas. She'd retired from cruise ships for good but there was a new resort opening on Lovango Cay and she thought she might head up housekeeping there. But then she'd heard from Xavier, who told her what he'd done—bought a hotel, sight unseen, on the island where she now lives.

Xavier is like a schoolboy doing handstands and backflips to capture Magda's attention, only in his case, the acrobatics are displays of his wealth—the way he managed to get the renovation done so quickly, the thousand-dollar bonuses for the staff. And sending the orchids that morning! (Vandas are Magda's favorite flower, as Xavier well knows.) She'd left them on her desk; if she brought them home, she would be asked all kinds of questions that she had no intention of answering.

Magda slips out of the hotel and climbs into her brand-new Jeep Gladiator, which is part Jeep, part pickup truck, and a convertible to boot. Her brother, William, had given her *quite* a look when she drove it home from Don Allen Ford; he was certainly wondering how she'd paid for it. She said, "I've lived on ships for so long that all I ever dreamed about was a new car, so I splurged." If he wasn't exactly satisfied with her explanation, that was his problem.

Magda has errands to do. She stops first at Hatch's for a fresh bottle of Appleton Estate 21 rum—she constantly seeks out reminders of the Caribbean—and, because she can't help herself, she also buys a ten-dollar scratch ticket. When she gets back out to her car, she scrapes the silver coating off with a dime from her change purse.

Ha! She's won five hundred bucks! She'll go back in to collect it next time.

She considers stopping by Bayberry Properties to see if Fast Eddie has any more listings for her to check out. But she doesn't like the way Eddie's sister, Barbie, looks at her, so she decides to send Eddie a text.

Please don't forget about me, Mr. Pancik, she writes.

To his credit, Eddie responds right away: I could never forget you, Magda! I'll circle back later this week with a list, as we discussed.

Magda loves William and Ezekiel to pieces but it's time she got her own place, especially now that it looks like she's staying.

She has one more errand to run—the Nantucket Meat and Fish Market. Magda wants to get soft-shell crabs; she'll sauté them in brown butter and serve them with dirty rice and roasted asparagus. The market is pleasantly chilly and smells like coffee; it houses the only Starbucks concession on the island. Magda heads for the bounty of the long, refrigerated butcher case, where she finds impeccable trays of rib eyes, individual beef Wellingtons, steak tips in three different marinades, chicken breasts stuffed with spinach and cheese, plump rainbows of vegetable kebabs, baby back ribs, lamb chops, lobster tails, jumbo shrimp cocktails, cilantro-lime salmon, and swordfish steaks as thick as paperback books. The line at the case is four or five people long but Magda doesn't mind waiting. It's the first time she's stopped moving all day.

The hotel has turned out beautifully, she has to admit; but of course, Xavier never does anything halfway. *If you're not planning on being the best, why do anything at all?* Isn't that what Xavier said the night she met him a million years ago, back when he first bought the cruise line? He'd addressed the staff in the Tropicana theater; everyone had been thrilled, Magda included, because it was an hour of free drinks. Magda can still picture Xavier, upright and self-important in his bespoke suit. That was over thirty years ago now, the night her fortune changed.

Xavier is coming to the island in August. Magda will make sure his suite is spotless.

Just thinking these words makes Magda laugh—which attracts the attention of the young man standing in front of her. He turns around.

"Oh," he says. "Hey, Ms. English."

For the love of Pete, Magda thinks. It's her long shot. She has a hard time coming up with the boy's name even though she spent all day with him, showing him how to vacuum in neat rows, how to scrub the oyster-shell tiles with an electric toothbrush. They'd covered a surprising amount of ground, though it was immediately clear the child had never so much as cleared his plate from the dinner table. They still have the laundry to tackle—folding a fitted sheet; will he ever master it? They also need time to go over the sensitive things maids come across—sex toys and props for role-playing, birth control pills, condoms, diaphragms, tubes of lubricant, falsies, and drugs and drug paraphernalia. She doesn't want him to be shocked.

"Hello..." She can't for the life of her remember his name. Did she use it today? She must have. Her mind grapples for it the way her hand feels around on her nightstand for her glasses in the dark of the early morning.

"Chad," he says.

She starts giggling. She can't help it. She bows her head and chortles into her cleavage, her body rocking with laughter. It's so *funny,* not only her forgetting his name when she was *with him all day* but also the name itself, Chad, when he appears, outwardly anyway, to be precisely that Nantucket type. A Chad named Chad. Magda laughs so hard, her stomach muscles ache and tears leak out of the corners of her eyes. Chad is staring at her, as are a couple of other people in line, which begins to sober her, but then Magda catches a glimpse of Chad's expression and it's so *befuddled* that Magda doubles over again. She's making a ticking noise that doesn't even sound like laughter, but it's all she can eke out. She's probably thirty seconds away from someone calling an ambulance.

Now it's Chad's turn to step up to the counter and order. He asks for three Wagyu fillets, and although Magda has known the boy for less than twelve hours, this is exactly what she would have guessed his family eats for dinner. Magda is finally able to catch her breath and compose herself, though little bursts of laughter continue until Chad turns around with his wrapped parcel and smiles uncertainly at her. "See you tomorrow, Ms. English," he says.

"See you tomorrow, Long Shot," she says. His smile widens; he can take a little ribbing, and Magda feels a pulse of optimism. She wonders if her gamble might work out after all.

* * *

Edie steps out of the meeting and thinks, *Is it just me or has this day been three weeks long?* She checks her phone.

There's a Venmo request for five hundred dollars from her ex-boyfriend.

No, Edie thinks.

This feels like a mistake or a joke, but a chill runs through her.

Graydon is out in the parched, cracked desert of Arizona; he accepted the job with Ritz-Carlton at its Dove Mountain property, the job they applied for together and planned to take together. But then things with Graydon got weird and awful and Edie changed her mind about the Ritz and decided to come home instead. Graydon, who by that point was *obsessed* with Edie, asked if he could come to Nantucket too—he said he would live with Edie and her mother, Love—but Edie said she didn't think that was a good idea. What she meant was that she didn't *want* Graydon on Nantucket. What she meant was that she wanted to break up. Edie had assumed she would work at the Beach Club like both her parents had, until her mother offhandedly mentioned that the Hotel Nantucket—which had been an eyesore and a blight throughout Edie's childhood—was undergoing a rumored thirty-million-dollar renovation. Edie wanted to be part of a team restoring a historic hotel to its former glory. And she would be safe; the waters surrounding the island would be nearly amniotic, protecting her from Graydon.

Except that now, here he is in her Venmo requests.

A couple walks across the lobby, dressed for dinner. Edie has nearly forgotten that there are guests in the hotel other than Kimber Marsh, her children, and their pit bull. It's the Katzens, Edie thinks, on their way to Cru; they wave as they head out the door. If Edie were playing her A-game, she would walk out with the Katzens, chat them up; after all, she had told Lizbet in her interview that the most important aspect of hospitality was making a connection with each and every guest at the hotel. But she does nothing and says nothing because she has a trash fire on her phone. *Five hundred dollars!*

She walks home to Sunset Hill, thinking there's no way she's going to let Graydon blackmail her. She deletes the Venmo request. He has some nerve!

A text comes in. Edie hopes it's her mother saying the Tater Tot Hotdish is ready. But when Edie checks, she sees the text is from Graydon: an emoji of a movie camera.

She has to pay him.

But she can't. She has a student-loan payment due on June 15 that's nearly half of her first paycheck.

She *won't* pay him! Who will he send the videos to? She's not famous; the *National Enquirer* doesn't care about her. And their mutual friends are woke enough that they'll realize Graydon is using his white-male privilege to get back at Edie for breaking up with him. They'll delete the videos without watching them (she hopes) and cancel Graydon.

But what if Graydon sends the videos to her *mother?* Can Edie risk *that?* Love had had Edie when she was forty. Now she's sixty-two years old, and although she tries to stay current—she knows who Billie Eilish and Doja Cat are—she doesn't quite understand the new sexual norms or the ways that Gen Z live their lives on their phones. Love probably doesn't think that Edie's still a virgin, but as close as they are, they never discuss sex. Nooooooo! (Edie binged the second season of *Euphoria* with her bedroom door not only closed but locked.) If Love saw Edie in the videos that Edie had allowed Graydon to take, she would die inside. Edie is Love's pride and joy, her prize and treasure, and her obsession with Edie has grown only more intense since Vance died. The worst thing would be if Love blamed *herself* for those videos, thinking that she didn't raise Edie right or set a good example.

Edie Venmos Graydon the five hundred dollars, which is most of what she has in her bank account—it's her graduation money. She wants to scream into the beautiful June afternoon, but she's afraid one of her neighbors on Sunset Hill will hear her.

She gets another text. From Graydon, of course. Ty! it says. With the thumbs-up emoji.

The last person to leave the break room is the one Grace most wants to see leave: Alessandra Powell. Grace hovers above as Alessandra drops four quarters into the jukebox (these are quarters that Grace watched Alessandra lift from petty cash) and picks songs—all of them the devil-worshipping heavy metal of the 1980s. Wow, Grace hasn't missed this music at all. She tries to spook Alessandra, positioning herself so that her figure in the white robe and Minnesota Twins cap might be reflected in the Plexiglas of the pinball machine that Alessandra has started playing. Grace does a little headbanging dance to amuse herself and get Alessandra's attention. Does Alessandra see her? No; she remains wholly focused on keeping the silver ball in play. Grace blows cold air down the back of Alessandra's neck, but she doesn't seem to notice that either. This can mean only one thing—the girl has demons inside her. Grace can practically hear their taunts: *You can't scare us! Nothing scares us!*

A second later, Grace realizes she's not the only one suspicious of Alessandra. There's someone else lurking just inside the door.

Lizbet isn't worried about the private life of Zeke or Adam or Chad or Edie, and she certainly isn't worried about Magda.

Alessandra is another story.

Right before the staff meeting, Mack Petersen from the Nantucket Beach Club called to congratulate Lizbet on opening day and ask how things were going. Mack did this in good faith despite the fact that they're direct competitors—Lizbet knows Mack from her days at the Deck. She couldn't keep herself from bragging, "I have Sweet Edie on my desk."

"You know I'm envious. She's my godchild."

"And I ended up hiring that woman Alessandra? The one who had been working in Italy?"

Mack said, "I'm not sure who you mean."

"Wasn't she supposed to interview with you? Alessandra Powell? For your front desk?"

Mack said, "I didn't have any front-desk positions open this year. The only position I hired someone for was night bell. I got lucky and nearly my entire staff from last year returned."

"Oh," Lizbet said. She was stymied for a second. Hadn't Alessandra said she was interviewing with Mack at the Beach Club? She had. She told Lizbet that Mack had basically offered her a position on the desk! "Well, let's hope I get that lucky next year."

Alessandra had lied, and that didn't feel great. Lizbet should have been more guarded during their interview, but Alessandra had charmed her—bringing Lizbet a sandwich when she knew she was interviewing right before lunch. How canny! How clever! (How manipulative!) And then she'd dodged the questions about her references. This manager retired, this one died, there is no one in all of Europe who can vouch for my performance. Lizbet had called all four of the hotels listed on the résumé, and only at one hotel—the Grand Hotel Tremezzo—had she found someone who could verify that yes, Alessandra Powell had worked there for two years, but no, nobody was around at that moment who had known Alessandra personally. Lizbet left messages at the other three hotels and is waiting for them to call back—though what is she going to do now? Fire Alessandra? The woman is exceedingly professional on the desk, and she's stunning to look at. She's beautiful enough to get away with murder.

* * *

Lizbet is about to start her shift on the night desk (they *need* a night auditor!) when she realizes she saw everyone on her staff leave the hotel except Alessandra.

Lizbet cracks open the door to the break room. Alessandra is standing at the pinball machine gyrating her hips like she's making love to the thing, and the machine is dinging and flashing its lights like it's enjoying it. The jukebox is playing "Same Old Situation" by Mötley Crüe, which Lizbet hasn't heard since she listened to 92 KQRS back in the Twin Cities growing up.

When the game is over—Alessandra must be pretty good, because it lasts longer than half the men Lizbet has been with—and the song changes to "Highway to Hell" by AC/DC (nearly every song on the jukebox is from the previous century), Alessandra steps up to the soft-serve ice cream machine and swirls herself a gigantic bowl of chocolate. She digs in like she hasn't eaten in days.

"Hey," Lizbet says, stepping into the room.

Alessandra blinks. Her wavy apricot-colored hair falls over one shoulder.

"We haven't really had a chance to chat," Lizbet says.

"Chat?" Alessandra says. Her spoon hovers over the peak of ice cream.

Lizbet considers confronting Alessandra with her lie about Mack and the Beach Club, but she doesn't, because the fact is, she can't afford for Alessandra to get defensive and quit. "I thought maybe we could get to know each other a little?" Lizbet hears how hokey this sounds, even pandering, as though she's sucking up to the most popular girl at school. *Can we please be friends?* She changes tacks. "Would you like me to call you an Uber? Where are you living?"

"I don't need an Uber, I can walk. I'm living on Hulbert Avenue."

Hulbert Avenue? Lizbet thinks. That's the most exclusive address in town; all of those homes front the harbor. "Nice," Lizbet says. "Are you *renting* on Hulbert?"

"I have a friend with a house," Alessandra says.

"I didn't realize you knew anyone here."

"It's a new friend." Alessandra holds Lizbet's gaze and licks ice cream off the back of her spoon. "Someone I met on the boat over here."

Whaaaa? Lizbet thinks. Alessandra met someone *on the boat* and now has a place to live on Hulbert? "Wow, lucky you," Lizbet says. Her voice sounds a little arch, so she tries to soften it. "How was your first day?"

Alessandra gives Lizbet a pointed look that seems to say, *Please go away and leave me to my ice cream.* "It was a day."

Lizbet changes into white jeans, a hydrangea-blue blouse, and—ahh—a pair of running shoes. She steps out to the desk and observes evening settling over the lobby. Golden, syrupy sunlight pours in through the open front doors, and guests head out to dinner—though, of course, not as many guests as Lizbet would like. The lobby feels a bit like a badly attended party. What can she do to increase occupancy? The hotel isn't cheap—it *shouldn't* be cheap—but it's slightly less expensive than their competitors are. Lizbet decides to reach out to every media outlet, all those places that fawningly covered the Deck. It would be nice to have some help from Xavier, but he doesn't seem concerned that their numbers are low. He cares only about the fifth key.

Kimber Marsh's son, Louie (the name completely suits the little dude; in his seersucker shorts and pressed white polo, he's both cute and formal, like a child king), wanders into the lobby alone, settles at one of the chessboards, and begins moving pieces. Lizbet watches him for a second, wondering if Kimber will appear. Mr. and Mrs. Stamm from room 303 stop by him on their way out the door.

"You really know what you're doing," Mr. Stamm says to Louie. "How old are you?"

Louie doesn't look up. "Six and a half."

Mr. Stamm chuckles and says to his wife, "A prodigy."

Louie moves his white rook and says, "Checkmate." He turns to Mr. Stamm. "Do you want to play?"

Mr. Stamm laughs. "I'm on my way out right now, but maybe tomorrow, how about that?"

Louie shrugs and the Stamms leave. Lizbet considers going over and offering to play with Louie, but then she sees the break-room door open and Alessandra slip out. Lizbet gets a nutty idea that she immediately dismisses. She's losing her mind; she's been at the hotel for nearly twelve hours and she has to last until midnight.

But…she deserves a quick break, and she's the boss, so there's no one to stop her.

Alessandra heads down the front stairs and pulls a bike off the rack—it's one of the hotel bikes; has she asked if she can use it? Lizbet approaches Raoul, who is posted by the front door and has the upright bearing of a guard at Buckingham Palace. "Do you mind watching the desk for twenty minutes or so while I get some air?"

"Not at all," Raoul says. Raoul has an old-school gallantry that Lizbet just adores and she briefly congratulates herself on a good hire.

"Little Louie is inside playing chess and I don't see his mother, so if you don't mind keeping an eye on him?" She winces. "I know you're not a babysitter."

"Happy to," Raoul says.

"Do you play chess?" Lizbet asks.

"I do, actually," Raoul says. "If it's quiet, maybe I'll let him beat me."

"Terrific! Thank you!" Lizbet watches Alessandra pedal off down Easton Street. "I'll be right back."

Lizbet also grabs a hotel bike—they're brand-new white Treks; Xavier bought a fleet of thirty-five—and takes off behind Alessandra. She savors the wind in her face, the softness of the air, and the gilded tone of the lowering sun, trying to ignore the fact that what she's doing is completely unhinged. She's following Alessandra home. If someone were filming this from above, they would see two women—in identical outfits!—one surreptitiously pursuing the other. The tail of Lizbet's blue blouse billows out behind her. She hums the Wicked Witch's theme music in her head.

Alessandra goes all the way down Easton, past Great Point Properties, past the entrance to Children's Beach, past the White Elephant, and Lizbet trails at a distance. She catches a whiff of garlic and butter coming from the Brant Point Grill and her stomach rumbles; she hasn't eaten a thing all day. Alessandra passes all the grand waterfront homes on the right and takes the curved left turn onto Hulbert before the Coast Guard Station and the Brant Point Light. Lizbet follows. A few cars pass, and Lizbet is afraid she'll see someone she knows. A bunch of customers from the Deck live on Hulbert; she and JJ used to be invited out here to private pool parties and croquet matches all the time. They'd become friends with two couples, the Bicks and the Laytons, both of whom live in this neighborhood. The Bicks' house, which has a tennis court, is up ahead and…Alessandra slows down.

There's no way that Alessandra is living at the Bicks' house, is there? Michael and Heidi are the quintessential golden couple—they're both tall, lean, and blond—and they have four young tow-headed children. Maybe Alessandra has struck some kind of deal where she watches the kids in the evenings in exchange for housing? But that doesn't feel quite right. Heidi has a full-time nanny. And something about the way Alessandra said, *I have a friend with a house…a new friend. Someone I met on the boat* was sexual in nature. Lizbet *thought* Alessandra was intimating that she'd met a guy on the boat, the guy invited her back to his house, and now she's living there.

Alessandra stops, swings her leg off her bike, and turns around. "Are you *following* me?" she says.

Lizbet's foot slips off the pedal and the bike wobbles, but Lizbet pulls the handlebars straight, hits the brakes, and doesn't crash.

She has no idea what to say. She considers chastising Alessandra for taking a hotel bike without asking, but that seems petty. "I saw you head out and I decided I could use a ride as well. It's such a beautiful evening and I have to work the desk tonight." Lizbet glances at the Bicks' house. The gate to the tennis court is ajar and there's a racket lying on the bench, so the Bicks must be back on island. Lizbet dearly hopes they aren't watching this exchange from their window. She started out the day strong, but now she has devolved into some kind of psycho-boss who follows her employees home. With great awkwardness, Lizbet wheels her bike around. "See you tomorrow." She pedals away, fighting the urge to check where Alessandra is headed. She tells herself it's none of her business.

When she arrives back at the desk, she finds Raoul and Louie deeply involved in a chess match. Raoul looks up with wide eyes. "The kid is whupping my butt. Fair and square."

Lizbet nods, preoccupied with her embarrassment. What must Alessandra think of her? It's mortifying—and yet Lizbet still feels that something isn't right, something bigger than lying about an interview (that could be seen as strategic) and bigger than taking a bike without asking (who cares; she'll bring it back tomorrow). Once Lizbet assures herself that nothing pressing needs her attention, she retrieves her cell phone from her office and surreptitiously slides it next to her computer, even though this is, by her own decree, forbidden. She sends a text to Heidi Bick: Hey, girl, just thinking of you. Are you on island? Now that I'm not working at the Deck, we can actually go out to dinner this summer! Let me know when you're free so we can catch up.

She hits Send and takes a breath. Then she decides to place another ad for a night auditor in the *Nantucket Standard* classifieds—she won't be able to go anywhere or do anything until she hires someone. This time, she lists the pay: *$25 per hour, plus possible bonuses!* Hopefully, that will do the trick.

Suddenly, a young woman is at the desk, holding out a white cardboard box. It's Beatriz from the Blue Bar.

"Chef asked me to deliver this to you with his compliments," she says.

Chef, Lizbet thinks. *Mario Subiaco.* She recalls that morning, JJ's proposal, the fruit frenzy on the zebrawood cutting board, and the cocktail. She could really use that cocktail now.

"Thank you!" Lizbet says. She opens the top of the box and nearly swoons.

"It's called the bakery box," Beatriz says. "One of Chef's specialties. Clockwise, you have homemade pizza rolls, gougères filled with béchamel, and two favorites from the Blue Bistro—savory rosemary and onion doughnuts and pretzel bread served with his signature honey mustard."

Sweet lightning! Lizbet thinks. "This looks...amazing."

"Chef wanted to be sure you ate something delicious today," Beatriz says, and she vanishes through the door that leads back into the bar. Lizbet hears laughter and chatter and Nat King Cole singing "Unforgettable." It sounds...fun. And lively. Lizbet feels a pang; despite her bravado, she misses the restaurant business.

She isn't sure where to start—she wants to inhale the whole box of goodies, but she picks up one of the two glistening, golden-brown doughnuts because she has heard stories about them. *Gah!* The doughnut is so good that Lizbet's eyelids flutter closed and she has to keep herself from moaning. Next, she nibbles the end of one of the flaky triangular pizza rolls and finds it chock-full of crumbled sausage and pepperoni in a sauce that's slightly spicy. It's so *insanely delicious* that she feels guilty. She casts a glance at Raoul and Louie. Raoul stands up and announces, "I should get back to my post." Louie returns the pieces to their home squares. Raoul swings by the desk and says, "That kid is something else. I thought I would let him win and he *killed* me."

Oh so reluctantly, Lizbet offers Raoul the box. "Would you like a doughnut or some pretzel bread?" She dearly hopes he doesn't take a gougère, because there are only three.

Raoul waves the box away. "Thank you, but I don't eat carbs."

Ha! Brilliant! Raoul heads back to the bell stand and Lizbet absconds with her box of treasure to her office but keeps an eye on Louie through the doorway. He starts another game against himself, but then Wanda appears, holding a notebook and a pencil, and says, "Mom wants you back in the suite, Louie, come on."

"In a minute," Louie says. "I'm playing."

Wanda puts her hands on her hips like an aggrieved mother. "You have a board in the room." Louie sighs, then follows his sister down the hall.

Lizbet pops a gougère into her mouth and it explodes with creamy béchamel. *Not bad, Subiaco,* she thinks. She remembers the night fifteen years earlier when JJ asked her to help him with some recipe development. He was trying to perfect an oyster pan roast, and Lizbet sat on a high stool in the kitchen at the Deck while JJ hand-fed her a plump, briny raw oyster, then a spoonful of the pan sauce (cream, bacon, thyme). This led to their first kiss, which led to them dating, then sleeping together, then, at the end of the summer, living together, and then to them buying the cottage on Bear Street and running the restaurant side by side until she discovered the pornographic texts on his phone. If anyone knows the dangers of being seduced by food, it's Lizbet Keaton.

And yet…she tears off a hunk of pretzel bread and swipes it lavishly through the honey mustard. She can't stop.

She decides to take a picture of the bakery box and send it to JJ; he'll be jealous and think she's gloating (she is). But when Lizbet picks up her phone, she sees a text from Heidi Bick.

Hey, girl, sorry, I was scooping Hayford from jiu-jitsu practice. I'm still in Greenwich, I leave for the island a week from Friday after the kids finish school. Michael has been up there for a couple months already working on a top secret project that requires complete silence, which cannot, of course, be found at home. I'm free any night after the eighteenth—it will def be Michael's turn to hang with the kids! Maybe you can get us into the Blue Bar? I heard it's going to be the new hot spot! Love u xoxo

Lizbet blinks. Heidi is back in Connecticut with the kids, and Michael has been on the island for a couple of months "working on a top secret project"? That doesn't mean he's sleeping with her front-desk manager, Lizbet tells herself. Being cheated on has destroyed Lizbet's faith in humanity; she automatically thinks the worst of everyone. It wasn't clear that Alessandra was pulling into the Bicks' house; that was just where she stopped to confront Lizbet. It was as if she had eyes in the back of her head. It was a little scary, to be honest.

Lizbet said she wanted to know everyone's secrets, but she understands now that she doesn't. She pops another gougère into her mouth. She doesn't at all.

7. Bad Reviews

June 15, 2022

From: Xavier Darling (xd@darlingent.co.uk)

To: Employees of the Hotel Nantucket

Good day, team. We have a sticky situation on our hands, I'm afraid. The reviews of our property on TravelTattler for the first week were primarily negative. Now, I understand that people are more likely to leave a review when they have a problem and that it's highly likely that all the guests who didn't leave a review left the hotel feeling perfectly content and satisfied with their stay. However, I will not be awarding the thousand-dollar bonus this week.

I hope you all realize that a satisfied guest isn't enough. I want you, please, to make every effort to see that our guests leave jubilant, energized, and inspired to tell the internet about their unparalleled stay at the Hotel Nantucket.

This is not meant as punishment or even a reprimand. Please think of this e-mail as an impetus to take your guest-service skills to the next level.

> Thank you.
>
> XD

TRAVELTATTLER REVIEWS

The Hotel Nantucket, Nantucket, Massachusetts

Dates of your stay: June 11–13

Number of people in your party: 3

Name (optional):

Please rate the following areas of the hotel on a scale of 1 to 10

Reception/check-in: 10

Room cleanliness: 10

Style/decor: 10

Concierge: 10

Wellness center: 10

Pools: 10

Room service/minibar: 10

Overall experience: 2

Please feel free to leave additional comments about your stay, singling out any staff members who made your visit memorable.

I wish you had a category for rating the bell staff because that would answer the riddle of how my two gal pals and I could love everything about this hotel and still give it a two-star experience overall. The bellman who was on duty during our stay was not only full of himself but also incredibly rude, unfriendly, and unaccommodating. He ruined what was an otherwise wonderful experience. We also suspect he was behind some inexplicable phenomena that happened in our room on the final night of our stay. He should be fired promptly.

Grace has been watching the day-to-day activity at the hotel unfold with great interest, and although she's biased, she happens to think her crush Zeke English is doing a terrific job. He was a little awkward during the first week while he was learning the ropes—and admittedly, he's nowhere near as polished as Adam, who works with Zeke during the day, or Raoul, who works nights—but today is June 11, the start of week two, and Zeke has clicked into gear like a fine race car.

When Roger's Taxi pulls up to the front of the hotel and disgorges three very exuberant-looking women of a certain age, Adam nudges Zeke and says, "All yours, stallion," and Zeke strides over with his winning smile, shoulders back, to welcome the ladies to the hotel.

The ringleader of the three women introduces herself as Daniella, then turns to her two friends and says, "Look at this hottie, gals!"

Gals? Grace thinks. That term is straight out of 1977. It makes Grace think of Farrah Fawcett Majors, the Dallas Cowboy cheerleaders, and Charlie perfume (everyone staying in the hotel that year wore it).

The other two women are Claire (frumpy) and Alison (hippie-dippie). Claire tells Zeke that the three of them are from Florida and have come to the island to "whoop it up." (Again Grace wonders, *Who says that anymore?*) It's Daniella's fiftieth birthday—and they're also celebrating Daniella's shiny new divorce.

"I'm on the prowl!" Daniella crows. "Like only a woman who lost her orthodontist husband to one of his patients' mothers can be." Daniella is tall with ringlets of black hair down to her waist and a wide mouth. She's a not-quite Cher.

Oh, dear, Grace thinks. She sees trouble barreling down on Zeke like a freight train.

Zeke delivers the ladies' bags to suite 117 and displays its wonders—the sound system, the electric shades, the complimentary minibar. Daniella hands Zeke a hundred-dollar bill and asks him to stay for a beer.

"Thank you so much for the offer, ladies, but I'm on the clock for another five hours, so I'll have to take a rain check."

"We expect to see you later," Daniella says. She squeezes Zeke's biceps through his hydrangea-blue button-down. "Look at these *guns!*"

Alison, who has frizzled gray-blond hair and is wearing a tie-dyed sundress, shrieks, "Dani-*ella!*" Claire, who wears glasses and mom jeans, blinks at Zeke and says, "You are quite the snack," which actually makes Zeke laugh.

But he hightails it out of there.

Grace is relieved that Zeke gets off work before the ladies leave their room, buzzed from the bottle of Laurent-Perrier rosé they ordered from the Blue Bar, and head out to dinner at Lola. Claire briefly tries to flirt with Raoul, asking if he's taken, and Raoul deadpans perfectly that yes, he's married to Adam, the day bellman. That shuts them up!

The next morning, Grace sees Zeke arrive at the hotel not in his uniform, as usual, but in workout clothes. He heads down to the yoga studio...and Grace follows. There are eight or nine women stretching, in anticipation of Yolanda's barre class. When Yolanda takes her place at the front of the room, Grace sees Zeke melt a little.

Aha.

Grace can hardly blame him. Twenty-seven-year-old Yolanda Tolentino looks like Chrissy Teigen's little sister; she has tousled dark hair highlighted auburn, flawless skin, big brown eyes, and a deep dimple in her left cheek. Her body is trim, limber, flexible. Over the past few weeks, Grace has seen Yolanda sail through the lobby. Once, she stopped to talk to Lizbet and held a tree pose—foot tucked against opposite knee, hands held over her head like branches—which was unusual but also impressive. Another time, Yolanda was waiting for the elevator and executed a full-on backbend, which caused Mr. Goldfarb from room 202 to hiccup in surprise. Yolanda, Grace is happy to report, is as lovely on the inside as she is on the outside. And she must eat like a horse—she's back and forth between the yoga studio and the kitchen of the Blue Bar half a dozen times a day.

When Yolanda sees Zeke, she hurries over to get him set up at the barre with a ball, a looped resistance band, and two-pound hand weights.

"Um…" Zeke says, looking at the tiny lavender weights. "I've held burritos that weigh more than this."

"Feel free to switch them out for heavier ones," Yolanda says. "Just remember, I warned you. And unfortunately, I don't have any grippy socks that will fit you."

"Big feet," says a woman just walking in. It's Daniella; she's followed by Alison and Claire. "We know what *that* means, don't we, gals?"

No, this won't do, Grace thinks. She blows cold air down the back of Daniella's neck, and as she does so, she inhales the unmistakable scent of last night's tequila. Daniella doesn't notice the draft; possibly, she welcomes it. When Claire and Alison spot Zeke, they start furiously whispering.

Grace is embarrassed for them. She has seen fourteen-year-olds with more composure.

"Zeke is a barre virgin!" Daniella cries out. "Don't worry, I'll be right behind you, Zeke, admiring your form."

"Me too," Alison says. She's wearing leggings printed with rainbows and peace signs.

"I'm moving closer," Claire says. She has on a T-shirt that reads I DATE EVERYBODY.

Yolanda starts the music. "Ladies, let's try to focus." She lifts her leg while crossing her arms in front of her chest. Zeke follows suit; he can't lift his leg very high at all, or maybe he can but he's simply too enraptured by Yolanda, in her white leggings and her hydrangea-blue tank, with her hair in a thick braid hanging over one shoulder, to try very hard.

Leg lifts transition to planks on the yoga mats, followed by push-ups. Grace watches Zeke do all this with ease. When the class moves to the barre, Yolanda says, "Who's ready for a thigh party?"

Daniella hoots and raises her arms over her head, giving Zeke an unimpeded view of her chest; Grace notices that she has removed the pads from her yoga top so that Zeke can see her nipples protruding.

"Heels together, toes apart," Yolanda says. "Now sink down six inches and find your high diamond."

Zeke tries to approximate the position but his heels lift only an inch off the ground; when he sinks down, he winces. "Up an inch," Yolanda says, "and down an inch. Remember, an inch is the size of a paper clip." When they "press down to finish," Zeke's legs shake uncontrollably; it's the funniest thing Grace has seen in a long time.

"End of the first set," Yolanda says. "Two to go."

Zeke looks longingly at the door.

"Everyone grab your balls," Yolanda says.

Daniella rolls her tongue. "Now you're talking," she says.

When barre class ends, there's a standoff. Zeke seems to want to chat up Yolanda, but Daniella, Alison, and Claire are clearly lingering in order to talk to Zeke.

Yolanda says, "Thanks for coming, everyone. I'm going to run to the restaurant for an acai bowl before I teach yoga. Ta!"

Daniella, Alison, and Claire close in on Zeke, who has his back up against the barre.

"Tonight's my birthday dinner at Ventuno," Daniella says. "Then we're going to the Club Car to sing and hopefully to the Pearl for a nightcap."

"Guess what we're giving Daniella for a present?" Claire says.

Zeke tells the ladies he can't begin to guess.

"You!" Alison says. "Please join us. We'll pay for everything."

"Wish I could, ladies," Zeke says. "But I have to work tonight."

"That's okay," Daniella says. "There's always the after-party."

Zeke is a sitting duck when the ladies from suite 117 enter the lobby that evening in a flurry of high-pitched cackling and waves of perfume. The three of them are dressed in sequins and feathers and high heels with red soles. Daniella is wearing a tiara.

Zeke takes a visible breath. He's such a good sport, Grace thinks. "Here's my birthday queen!" Zeke says, taking Daniella's hand and allowing her to twirl. "Love the Louboutins."

The ladies scream. "He knows about Louboutins!"

Alison says, "Let's get a selfie. Daniella, you stand next to Zeke."

Daniella crushes herself against one side of Zeke, and Claire does the same on the other side while Alison, on the far side of Claire, holds her phone out in front of them. "Everyone say, 'Duck…duck…goose!'" She presses the button at the same time that both Daniella and Claire squeeze Zeke's butt cheeks.

"Whoa!" Zeke says, raising his arms and stepping back.

What? Grace thinks. It might be time for her to show her resting-bitch face on Claire's phone screen. These ladies are Out. Of. Line!

At that moment, Roger's Taxi pulls up and the ladies pile in; as the car pulls away, they wave at Zeke out the open window.

Grace dearly hopes that by the time Daniella, Alison, and Claire return, Zeke will be off work and safely home in bed. But at just a couple of minutes to midnight, Daniella stumbles up the stairs in her heels. Claire, behind her, is holding her shoes in her hand, and Alison is still down on the sidewalk doing some kind of psychedelic dance to music apparently only she can hear.

They're drunk, Grace thinks. *As blotto as Dahlia Benedict used to get, back in the good old days.*

"Hey, ladies," Zeke says. His voice is weary. "How was the birthday?"

Daniella snakes an arm around Zeke's waist and snuggles against him. "We have a proposition for you."

The church bells in town toll midnight. "All propositions will have to wait until tomorrow, ladies. I'm getting off my shift and I'm beat. I'll see you in the morning."

"Oh no, you don't!" Daniella says, her tone of voice serrated now. "We're calling in that rain check. Come upstairs and have champagne with us," she says, pulling him out of the lobby.

"Don't be afraid," Alison says. "We don't bite."

"Speak for yourself," Claire says.

Daniella pulls five hundred-dollar bills out of her purse. "We'll tip you for your excellent service."

Zeke holds up his palms. "I'm sorry, ladies." He takes careful steps backward into the lobby, which is deserted. *I'm here, Zeke,* Grace thinks. *I'm here.* "I have to get home now. You all have a good night, and happy birthday, Daniella."

"It's my fiftieth birthday," Daniella says. "Just come up for ten minutes."

Absolutely not, Grace thinks. She needs to get help. She widens her scope and sees the answer just on the other side of the door that leads to the Blue Bar. Grace ever so gently puts a hand on Yolanda's back.

"Hey, Zeke!" Yolanda steps into the lobby, holding a takeout box. She's wearing a stretchy black catsuit, a porkpie hat, and a pair of Chuck Taylors. She waves at the ladies and slips her arm through Zeke's. "Would you mind walking me out to my car?"

Zeke exhales. "Of course. I was just leaving myself. Good night, ladies."

"But…" Daniella says.

Zeke and Yolanda step out onto the front porch. Daniella, Alison, and Claire stare after him.

"Thank you," Zeke whispers to Yolanda.

"You don't have to walk me anywhere," Yolanda says, pointing across the street to a vintage metallic-green Bronco with a white top. She smiles up at him, revealing the cute dimple. "I had the most incredible meal at the Blue Bar tonight. Have you eaten there yet?"

"Uh…"

Yolanda sighs. "I'm madly in love with the chef."

"You are?" Zeke says.

She's in love with Mario Subiaco? Grace thinks. *Well, that explains why she spends so much time in the kitchen.*

Yolanda skips down the stairs with a wave. "Have a good night, Zeke." She drives off, and Zeke stares after her. He turns around to see the backlit figure of Daniella standing in the lobby. She crooks a finger at him, but Zeke runs for home. *Good night, sweet prince!* Grace thinks.

Then she follows the ladies to suite 117.

Claire passes out facedown on the bed in the second bedroom. *She's going to miss all the fun,* Grace thinks. Alison declares she's drawing herself a bath, and in a few moments the tub is filled with steaming water. She takes the box of matches from the little table next to the tub and tries to light the lemon-and-mint candle, but the match sputters and goes out. She tries a second match but it happens again. And again. She can't get a match to stay lit. She turns on the pearly light around the mirror, and this sets a similar mood, so she steps one foot into the tub.

She shrieks. The water is ice cold. And then the light goes out.

"Daniella!" she cries.

Daniella is in the master bedroom trying to make the electronic shade go down. Every time she pushes the button to lower the shade, the shade starts to go down, but then, as if it changed its mind, it travels back up. Grace is delighted! The petals of the lilies and peonies in the Surfside Spring bouquet wither and fall to the table, and while Daniella is gasping at this, Grace whips the shade all the way up. Daniella picks up the phone to call the front desk, but there isn't a dial tone. She flops on the bed, still in her red-soled shoes, and pulls a pillow over her face. Grace goes into the sound system, and an instant later music is blaring: Quiet Riot's "Cum on Feel the Noize." Daniella sits bolt upright in bed, and Grace laughs and laughs. She hasn't had this much fun since *girls* were *gals*.

TRAVELTATTLER REVIEWS

The Hotel Nantucket, Nantucket, Massachusetts

Dates of your stay: June 12–15

Number of people in your party: 1

Name (optional): Franny Yates

Please rate the following areas of the hotel on a scale of 1 to 10

Reception/check-in: 1

Room cleanliness: 10

Style/decor: 10

Concierge: 10

Wellness center: 10

Pools: 10

Room service/minibar: 10

Overall experience: 5.5

Please feel free to leave additional comments about your stay, singling out any staff members who made your visit memorable.

I enjoyed my three-night stay at the Hotel Nantucket;

however, I'm only giving it five and a half stars overall because the night of my check-in was an unmitigated disaster, and had the hour not been so late and had every other room on the island not already been booked, I would have left immediately. The front-desk clerk and the night bellman were harried and distracted, and the front-desk clerk was, at one point, snippy with me. Then it took the night bellman thirty minutes to deliver my bags to my room when all I wanted to do was put on my pajamas and go to sleep. Furthermore, when the bellman came, he neglected to explain any features of the room. I didn't realize until my final day, while chatting with a lovely couple at the adult pool, that everything in the minibar was complimentary.

The Blue Bar, however, was outstanding and the perfect place to eat as a party of one. I went all three evenings of my stay. My compliments to the chef!

This review, forwarded to her by Xavier, is waiting in Lizbet's in-box when she gets to work on June 16. (She could easily check their TravelTattler reviews herself, but she's too busy overseeing operations at the hotel, and Xavier has a five-hour jump on the day, which feels like an unfair advantage.)

The comments accompanying this survey read as follows:

Good morning, Elizabeth—

After reading this survey, I checked the schedule and discovered that the night-desk clerk was you and that the night bellman was Raoul Wasserman-Ramirez. I suppose I don't need to mention that, as the GM, you must uphold our rigorous hospitality standards. The hotel isn't anywhere near full, so I would urge you to pay close attention to the guests who are in residence. The woman who wrote this review could easily have been Shelly Carpenter. Keep your eye on the fifth key, Elizabeth! The fifth key!

XD

Lizbet is starting to resent Xavier Darling. How dare he judge her when he's in London and she's here, chest-deep in the trenches. He *checked the schedule,* as though he's Big Brother. Bah! He can send all the admonishing e-mails he wants, but he isn't going to impress Shelly Carpenter or the second woman, whoever she is, if he doesn't help her deal with their staffing shortages and low occupancy.

Even so, Lizbet's indignation (and why can he not call her Lizbet like she's asked him to?) is mixed with guilt and culpability. That woman—Franny Yates of Trappe, Pennsylvania—checked in three hours late (not her fault; Cape Air was delayed due to fog) during a moment of crisis.

The crisis involved Wanda Marsh. The Marsh children had made themselves quite at home at the hotel. Every morning and every evening, Louie would come down to the lobby in a polo shirt buttoned to the top, his hair wet and combed, wearing his funny little glasses, and he would sit at a chessboard playing against himself, waiting for one of the guests to notice him and offer to play a game. Louie always won, and he became something of a curiosity, a six-and-a-half-year-old chess genius right there in the lobby of the Hotel Nantucket! One of the guests (Mr. Brandon, room 301) had written about Louie in his TravelTattler review, saying how much he'd enjoyed playing chess every morning with Louie while he drank his cup of percolated Jamaica Blue Mountain coffee. Lizbet was just waiting for Xavier to award Louie the thousand-dollar bonus.

Wanda wandered the hotel freely as well. She always had a Nancy

Drew mystery in her hand—she was working her way through them in chronological order, though her mother had only bought her up to number twelve, *The Message in the Hollow Oak,* and she was already on number nine, *The Sign of the Twisted Candles,* so she would soon be out of books. Wanda had also started carrying a spiral notebook and a number-two pencil because she wanted to write her own mystery novel starring girl sleuth Wanda Marsh. She was constantly asking people, staff and guests alike, if they had noticed anything strange or secret around the hotel, but the only mystery she'd learned of was the Case of the Disappearing Almond Croissants. It *was* unusual how rapidly Beatriz's croissants, filled with almond-flavored marzipan, vanished from the continental breakfast, and why didn't the kitchen ever make a second batch?

Unlike her children, Kimber Marsh was having a difficult time settling in. Back on the third night of their stay, Kimber had wandered down to the lobby at one in the morning. Lizbet was on the night desk.

"I suffer from chronic insomnia," Kimber said.

Lizbet nearly asked if they could switch places: Kimber could watch the desk and Lizbet would go to suite 114 and sleep in the emperor-size bed.

Kimber poured herself a giant cup of coffee—coffee?—and leaned against the desk to have a chat. *Fine, good,* Lizbet thought. It would keep her awake for her remaining hour.

Kimber said, "My husband left me for our nanny, whom he has now impregnated—and let me tell you, that was a wake-up call."

Yes, you told me, Lizbet thought. She'd had a wake-up call of her own, though she didn't want to tell Kimber Marsh about her breakup with JJ. She was so tired, she was sure she'd start to cry.

"I'm going to use this summer to reconnect with my kids," Kimber said. "I traveled so often for work, I barely saw them. They were always with Jenny, our nanny. Honestly, it's no wonder Craig left me for her. I was never around, so she slotted herself right into my vacant place and became not only a substitute mom but a substitute wife." Kimber leaned in. "That's why the kids are so consumed with the reading and the chess—something was missing from their little lives, and that something was me." Kimber sipped her coffee and reached for a copy of the Blue Book sitting on the desk. "Starting tomorrow, I'm going to do better. I'm going to do all the suggested itineraries in this guidebook."

The following day, Thursday, Kimber and the kids took Doug to Tupancy Links for a long walk, then they went to Barnaby's Place to do an art project, had lunch at Something Natural, and spent the afternoon on Children's Beach. But on Friday, Kimber plopped herself under an umbrella by the pool and read while Louie played chess in the lobby and Wanda interviewed hotel guests and Zeke took Doug out to do his business. On Saturday, Kimber didn't come down from her room until late afternoon. When she did, she had her laptop with her; she announced she was going to sit in the lobby and write her memoirs. *Okay?* Lizbet thought. At least Kimber could keep an eye on Wanda, who was finishing the last Nancy Drew mystery she had, and Louie, who was playing chess against himself. But Lizbet felt dismayed that the Marsh family had spent the entire day inside. Late-June days on Nantucket were the gold standard for the season—blue skies, plentiful sunshine, lilacs and cherry blossoms, and without the overbearing heat and humidity of July and August. But Sunday morning, Kimber rebounded and took the kids strawberry picking at Bartlett's Farm. When they came back, Wanda walked into the lobby proudly holding an overflowing quart of luridly red fruit. While Lizbet was pleased they had gotten out, she couldn't help thinking about the pristine white linens on the beds and the Annie Selke rug, so she offered to wash the strawberries and let the children eat them over soft-serve vanilla ice cream in the break room.

Both Wanda and Louie had been gobsmacked by the ice cream machine.

"I want to work here when I grow up," Wanda announced.

Then, at a quarter past ten on Sunday evening—when Lizbet was fading fast; she'd worked double shifts for seven straight days— Kimber Marsh came flying into the lobby in what Lizbet's mother would have called "a dither."

Wanda wasn't in her bed, she said. "Have you seen Wanda?" Kimber practically screamed. *"Have you seen her?"*

"I haven't," Lizbet said. She did a sweep of the lobby, checking Wanda's favorite reading chair and under the piano, where (inexplicably) Wanda sometimes liked to read, then said, "Let me look in the break room." (The allure of the soft-serve machine was strong; Lizbet had to fight it herself each and every day.)

But the break room was empty.

Lizbet enlisted Raoul's help—he would search the hotel, floor by floor. Kimber asked if it might be possible for her to let Doug out of their suite. She was certain he would lead them right to Wanda. Lizbet hesitated; the last thing she wanted was a pit bull roaming the halls of the hotel. But Lizbet sensed the urgency—an eight-year-old child was missing at ten fifteen at night—so she okayed it.

Raoul called up from the wellness center: no Wanda. "I thought she might be in the yoga room," Raoul said. "That fountain is mesmerizing." He was now moving to the first floor.

"Check all the unoccupied rooms, please," Lizbet said. There were twenty-one empty rooms and six empty suites (Lizbet felt each vacancy like a pinhole in her heart). "Maybe she found a way in."

Lizbet tried to think like Wanda. She seemed fascinated by the other guests, so Lizbet poked her head into the only populated area of the hotel, the Blue Bar—and wow! The place was popping. The bar was three-deep, every seat was occupied, the copper disco ball had dropped, and a group of people were dancing to "Tainted Love" in the space in front of the penny wall. Lizbet surveyed the crowd at hip level and tried to peer under tables. There was no sign of Wanda anywhere, though Lizbet spied plenty of people drinking flame-red cocktails, the Heartbreaker.

When Lizbet got back to the desk, a round, middle-aged woman wearing glasses with dark, square frames and a fanny pack around her waist—she looked like an aging version of Velma from *Scooby-Doo*—was standing at the desk.

"Finally!" she huffed.

"I'm so sorry," Lizbet said. "You must be Ms. Yates?"

"I arrived over five minutes ago and you're the first person I've seen!"

Lizbet returned to her spot behind her computer just as Raoul came rushing down the corridor, saying, "I'm headed up to the second floor."

Lizbet gave Raoul the thumbs-up; she was afraid if she spoke, she would lose her cool. A child missing in the hotel, she thought. Or *not* in the hotel. When was the right time to call the police?

"I'll need a form of ID and your credit card, please, Ms. Yates."

Franny Yates pulled both a Pennsylvania driver's license and a Mastercard out of her fanny pack.

"You're certainly traveling light," Lizbet said.

"My luggage is down on the sidewalk!" Franny said. "It's far too heavy for me to carry up the stairs. Silly me, I thought a hotel that costs as much as this one does might actually have a bellman!"

"We do have a bellman," Lizbet said. "Right now, he's assisting another guest. I'm happy to fetch your luggage."

"You won't be able to get it up the stairs," Franny said.

Lizbet winked at Franny. "You haven't seen me with kettlebells." But when Lizbet went to the hotel's entrance and looked down the staircase, she saw three black suitcases that were each big enough to contain a dead body. Franny Yates was staying at the hotel for only three nights. What could she possibly have packed?

Lizbet returned to the desk. "My apologies—you were absolutely correct. We'll have to wait for Raoul."

"How long will he be?" Franny asked, checking her phone. "I'd like to get to bed."

"Of course," Lizbet said. Just then, Raoul called. "She's not on the second floor, and Kimber says she and Doug checked the third floor and she's not there either. I'll sweep the fourth floor. You've checked the pools, yes?"

"Pools?" Lizbet said. She started to tremble. "No…"

"Oh, man," Raoul said.

Lizbet hung up. She held prayer hands up to Franny. "I'll be back in just a minute."

"But my room number? My key? My luggage is still on the sidewalk. What if someone takes it?"

"This is Nantucket," Lizbet said. "No one is going to touch it and it's too big for anyone to walk away with. I'll get your keys as soon as…" But Lizbet didn't finish the sentence. She hurried out the pool door, praying she wasn't going to see the small form of Wanda Marsh floating facedown. Both children could swim, she reminded herself. She hit the pool lights. No Wanda. She exhaled—but there was still the adult pool on the lower level and the hot tub. She recalled that Wanda was intensely curious about the Mystery of the Hot Tub, because it was restricted to people fourteen and older. Lizbet raced back through the lobby, passing Franny Yates, who had plopped herself cross-legged *on the floor* in front of the desk, which Lizbet understood was some kind of statement or protest, because there were armchairs and ottomans less than five feet away. "Be right—" Lizbet said. She ran down the stairs, through the wellness center, and out the door. The adult pool was dark and quiet.

"Wanda?" Lizbet whispered. She peered into the hot tub, feeling very much like the doomed heroine in a horror film.

It was empty.

Lizbet headed back upstairs, thinking she had dodged a huge bullet—Wanda hadn't drowned in the pools. Though Lizbet was growing more and more agitated. Where *was* she?

"Let me get your keys," Lizbet said to Franny Yates. "I'll upgrade you to a suite because you've been so patient. Here you go. Suite two fourteen. You can take either the stairs or the elevator to the second floor, and then it's all the way down the hall to the left."

"What about my *luggage?*" Franny Yates said.

"As soon as the bellman is free, I'll have him bring it to you."

"I want to go to sleep!"

"Ms. Yates, I need to ask for your indulgence. We have a situation here—"

"Your situation is that your hotel stinks," Franny Yates said. She marched off down the hall.

Lizbet wasn't sure what to do. Should she try to schlep Franny Yates's luggage up the stairs herself? Should she go up to the fourth floor to help look for Wanda? Should she call the police? *A child is lost.* Lizbet wasn't a mother but she understood how serious this was. Lizbet went down the stairs to the street and looked both ways. No Wanda.

She heard the phone ringing back in the lobby and she hustled up the stairs, taking them two at a time, so when she reached the top, her heart was pounding in her ears. "Hello?"

"We found her," Raoul said. "She was wandering around the fourth floor."

"Oh, thank God." Lizbet paused. "What was she doing *there?*" The fourth floor had odd roof angles and very small windows, and the Historic District Commission would have had to approve any structural changes that would be visible from the street, so Xavier had opted not to renovate it just yet. Lizbet had ventured up to the fourth floor only once; it was, essentially, a cavernous and dusty attic.

Raoul said, "She said she was looking for the ghost."

The ghost! Lizbet thought. She had been very careful never to mention the supposed ghost to anyone, and especially not Wanda, but Zeke might have let it slip.

"We have a check-in to suite two fourteen who is very anxious for her bags. There are three of them, and I would deliver them myself but they're each the size of a small home."

"I'll be down as soon as I'm finished cleaning up here."

"Cleaning up?" Lizbet said.

"Doug was so excited to see Wanda that he had an accident."

Lizbet closed her eyes. The other line of the hotel phone rang. It was suite 214. "You *have* to get suite two fourteen her luggage. Please, Raoul. Right now."

"But the dog—"

"Raoul, please!"

"Yes, boss," Raoul said.

Lizbet answered the other line. "Your luggage is on its way, Ms. Yates."

"You're a liar!" Franny Yates yelled. "I can see my luggage from my window. It's still on the sidewalk!"

Franny Yates's review is factually correct—it took Raoul a full thirty minutes to deliver her luggage, both Lizbet and Raoul were harried and distracted, and Lizbet was, perhaps, a bit snippy. But was the check-in an "unmitigated disaster"? No, an unmitigated disaster would have been Wanda staying missing or found dead.

Lizbet had comped Franny Yates's entire bill at the Blue Bar (three nights, two hundred and sixty dollars). Why didn't her review mention the comped meals?

Lizbet clicks out of the e-mail from Xavier and rests her head, ever so briefly, on her desk. It's seven thirty in the morning and she's so tired, she could sleep until seven thirty tomorrow morning. She's so demoralized, she feels like crying. Or crying uncle.

She needs a night auditor.

8. Lie, Cheat, and Steal

Grace tightens the belt of her robe and does her usual nocturnal sweep through the hotel, beginning with the room where Louie and Wanda are sleeping. They've been taking turns in each of the four bunks; tonight, they're both in uppers. Wanda has her note-pad tucked under her pillow, and Louie has fallen asleep in his glasses, clutching the white queen piece. Grace can hear Doug the dog snoring in the other room. He always lies in front of the door of the suite; if Grace goes anywhere near him, he'll wake up and snarl. Kimber, the mother, sleeps with her arms and legs in an X; she looks like a blue-and-green-haired angel fallen from the sky.

Grace floats out of suite 114 and pops in to check on the Belle-fleurs in room 306—*Oops, sorry to interrupt!*—then to suite 216, where Mrs. Reginella is scrolling through the text messages on her husband's cell phone, and then down to room 111, where Arnold Dash sleeps with the urn of his wife's ashes on the nightstand. Grace wishes there were more action. She hopes that as July gets closer, occupancy will increase. The hotel is so welcoming, the staff so attuned to every detail. What's keeping the guests away? Maybe there's too much competition or maybe it's too expensive. After all, when this was a "family-friendly budget hotel," it was jam-packed. Maybe the hotel's reputation is too damaged to rehabilitate. (Is that *her* fault?) She wonders what ever happened to the article that that lovely young woman, Jill Tananbaum, came to write. As far as Grace knows, it hasn't been printed.

Suddenly, Grace catches a whiff of something that smells like a passing garbage truck, and she realizes a new threat is about to enter the hotel. She swoops down to the lobby, which is warmly lit, with Norah Jones playing over the sound system. Lizbet is at her post at the desk, perusing summer dresses on the Alice and Olivia website. Grace can hear people in the Blue Bar, chanting "Don't! Stop! Believin'!," which is par for the course. The disco ball dropped over an hour ago.

Everything seems to be in order, but nevertheless, Grace's hackles are up. There's a predator approaching.

She hears footsteps on the stairs. A figure walks through the doors of the hotel.

Really? Grace thinks. *This guy?*

Lizbet is so tired when she interviews Richard Decameron—a fifty-four-year-old father of three from Avon, Connecticut, who has answered her prayers and applied for the job of night auditor— that the exchange has a dreamlike quality. He arrives at the hotel at ten thirty at night, fresh off the late ferry, but he's as ebullient and chipper as a QVC host trying to sell you the leaf blower that will change your life. He's dressed like it's casual Friday at the hedge-fund office, in a navy-blue spring suit, a navy-and-yellow-checked shirt, and chocolate suede Gucci loafers without socks. He has a dad bod—a bit of a paunch—and gray hair thinning on top, but his smile and his twinkling eyes are appealing. He gives Lizbet strong vibes of guys she knew in college, the fun, good-natured best friends of the hot-jock jerks everyone was in love with. Richard Decameron—he asks her to call him Richie—was the guy who actually stuck around to make sure you got in a cab after you did that last, ill-advised shot of tequila.

Lizbet prints out his résumé. He was an executive in the insurance business in Hartford for thirty years, and for the past two years, he's been working for something called Kick City.

"This...Kick City? I'm not familiar with it," Lizbet says.

"It's a sneaker-broker website," Richie says. "When athletes or rappers drop a limited-edition shoe, our brokers snap them up and resell them. I'm sure it sounds like kid stuff, but trust me, it's big business."

"What inspired you to make the switch?" Lizbet asks.

"I wanted a change from insurance, something with a little more sex appeal."

"And what brings you to Nantucket?"

Richie sighs. "I'm divorced, my ex-wife has recently started dating again, the new guy lives in the same town that I do, and it got claustrophobic, so I decided to treat myself to a summer at the beach. I'm a night owl by nature, so when I saw you advertising for a night auditor, I thought I'd reach out."

"Do you have housing?" Lizbet asks. *Please say yes,* she thinks. She wants a night auditor so badly, she might let Richie sleep in one of the empty rooms. (The rest of the staff would, no doubt, mutiny.)

"I'm staying at the hotel out by the airport tonight," he says. "Tomorrow I have an appointment with a woman who's renting a room in her home on Cliff Road."

"Ah, wonderful. And you're familiar with FreshBooks? You'll be fully responsible for preparing guest invoices..."

"I have all kinds of systems-software experience," Richie says. "I'm a numbers guy. I was a math major at UConn back in the day." He pumps a fist. "Go Huskies!"

She likes his energy, especially so late at night. "How comfortable are you with guest interaction?"

"I talk to everyone. My kids find it embarrassing."

"How old are your kids?" Lizbet is asking just to be polite. She's going to hire this guy.

"Kingsley is thirteen, Crenshaw is eleven, and Millbrook is eight." He pulls out his phone. "Here's a picture of our family in happier times."

Grace hovers above so that she can scrutinize the photo. There's a slightly younger version of Richie posing next to a pretty brunette with three smiling children arranged in front of them. There's a river, a waterwheel, trees aflame with color—it's autumn. The youngest child is holding a basket of apples.

This family looks happy. Grace notices Richie's hand trembling ever so slightly as he gives the phone to Lizbet, who beams at the photo. Is she, like Grace, wondering what happened to the marriage?

"Will your children get a chance to visit Nantucket this summer?" Lizbet asks.

"Haven't gotten that far yet," Richie says. "I'm just trying to get a viable situation in place."

"Well, if this helps, I'm happy to offer you the position of night auditor. It'll be six nights a week, I'm afraid. I can only cover one night and still keep my sanity."

"I'm happy to work seven nights," Richie says. "I'd prefer it. It'll keep me out of trouble. It's best that I keep busy so I don't miss my kids as much."

Lizbet exhales with obvious relief and looks right at the space that Grace is occupying. For the first time, Grace wonders if maybe Lizbet is supernaturally sensitive and can see a stolen hotel bathrobe and her missing Minnesota Twins cap floating in the air.

Definitely not, Grace thinks. The poor woman is merely exhausted. But even so, Grace rises a bit.

Lizbet says, "We have a family in suite one fourteen, a mother with two children. They're paying their bill in cash. You'll invoice them every week, and then Kimber, that's the mother, will bring down cash, which you can just keep in the safe until I find time to go to the bank to deposit it." She smiles. "I can trust you with the safe combination?"

Richie laughs. "My references will all vouch that I'm a perfectly average good-enough guy."

"Have you ever done any marketing?" Lizbet asks.

"I sat in on all the meetings at Kick City."

Lizbet frowns. "Occupancy at the hotel is below fifty percent, and I just don't understand why. The hotel was, admittedly, mediocre for a long time. I'm not sure if it's the lackluster reputation we're grappling with or..."

"Or?"

"Well, some people say there's a ghost."

Richie hoots. "The hotel is haunted? That's fantastic! I would think that would draw people to the hotel rather than keep them away. You should be promoting the ghost story."

"We should?" Lizbet says.

"Absolutely yes," Richie says. "Advertise the ghost! Market the ghost!"

Hmm, Grace thinks. There's still a stench coming off Richie Decameron—something's wrong; she can't say what—but she's willing to plug her nose and ignore it because it sounds like Richie is interested in her story. *Hello, Richie!* she calls out nasally, though of course he can't hear her. *I'm here! I was murdered!*

Everything Alessandra Powell owns fits into two (knockoff) Louis Vuitton duffels that she bought at the Mercato di Sant'Ambrogio in Florence.

Michael told Alessandra that his wife and children were due on island on June 18—but Alessandra had wormed her way so deeply into Michael's psyche that she thought, just maybe, he would decide to leave his wife. It would be quite a coup, though not her biggest (that would be Giacomo, who gave up both his runway-model mistress and his heiress wife for Alessandra). From what Alessandra can tell, Heidi Bick is the kind of wife and mother who meets her besties for yoga every morning after dropping the children off at their progressive and obscenely expensive private schools, then swings by the organic grocery on her way home so she can whip up whatever eclectic dish Sam Sifton has recommended that day in his *New York Times* cooking column. *(On Wednesday, maybe a tahdig…)* Heidi not only takes care of the four Bick children, she's also the point person for Michael's father, who has Parkinson's.

Alessandra met Michael Bick on the fast ferry back in early April. Alessandra had feared it would be slim pickings as far as male prospects were concerned—nearly all the men were sporting Carhartt's and work boots and dropping their *r*'s—but then Alessandra spied Michael with the Vacheron watch and his master-of-the-universe posture. At the ferry snack bar, he ordered a Sam Adams and a clam chowder, and Alessandra popped behind him in line and ordered the same. She took a seat one row over facing him and pulled out her well-worn copy of *The Sun Also Rises*. She drank her beer, let her chowder cool, and—surprise, surprise!—caught Michael staring at her.

"I'm sorry," he said. "It's not every day I see a beautiful woman drinking a beer and reading Hemingway."

By the end of the ride, Michael had moved into the seat across from Alessandra and bought them another round of beers; their respective chowders had gone untouched, and Alessandra's book lay facedown, forgotten. They had both stretched the truth about their situations. Michael said he was "taking some time apart from his wife," who was "back in Greenwich with the kids." Alessandra said she had been living in Europe for the past eight years and was "treating herself" to an American summer.

"The Riviera gets old after a while," she said, making them both laugh.

He invited her over to his place for a drink. She told him she had to check into her Airbnb (she didn't have one booked). He insisted, spinning her Cartier love bracelet and saying, "Unless your heart belongs to the person who gave you this?"

"Uh, *no,*" she said, regarding the bracelet as she might a hand-cuff. (Giacomo had given it to her a few weeks before he was sent to prison.)

"Great!" Michael said. "Then come for a drink."

"I really can't."

"Just one. Please?"

The house was more than Alessandra could have hoped for. It was one of the huge old family "cottages" right on the harbor that they'd passed on the ferry. It had a long, elegant pool that fronted their tiny private beach and a tennis court in the side yard. ("Do you play?" Michael asked. "A little," Alessandra said.) The inside of the house was tasteful and fresh, magazine-worthy—lots of white wainscoting and exposed blond beams and a massive stone fire-place and a table laden with silver-framed photographs (the wife he was supposedly taking some time apart from and the four children) behind the wide, deep sofa.

Michael kissed her outside on the deck, right away biting her lower lip. He wrapped his hand in a length of her hair, tugging a little to let her know who was in charge. (He, erroneously, thought this was him.) He slid his mouth down to her neck, lingering in the kill spot just below her ear; good boy, he'd been well trained by wifey, though Alessandra would bet a schmillion dollars he no longer kissed Heidi Bick this way. He unbuttoned

Alessandra's blouse slowly, his pinkie just barely grazing her nipple, and Alessandra felt a pulsing between her legs that was replicated by the ruby beacon of Brant Point Light in the distance.

He had her panting—shirt open, breasts exposed, jeans unzipped—when he turned and walked back into the house.

Alessandra waited a second, wondering if he was having a crisis of conscience. She chastised herself; she had made a poor choice.

When she finally followed him inside, she had to let her eyes adjust to the dark. There was milky moonlight through a window, blue numbers on a cable box—and then hands grabbed her waist and she screamed, genuinely frightened, and realized she wasn't in charge at all. She also realized Michael Bick had, very likely, brought home women he didn't know before. Possibly he did it all the time.

But in the pearl-gray light of morning—fog covered the harbor like a layer of dust on an antique mirror—Michael traced one of her eyebrows and said, "Where did you come from, Alessandra Powell?"

That was the question, wasn't it? Alessandra was originally from San Francisco, where her mother, Valerie, waited tables at the storied Tosca Café in North Beach. Valerie and Alessandra lived in a building down the street from the restaurant. Valerie kept their apartment clean, didn't drink too much (wine occasionally), and didn't do drugs (weed occasionally); there was always enough money for groceries and for Alessandra to get ice cream down on the pier or go to the movies or, when she was older, take the bus to Oakland and thrift-shop. But there was something a little off about Alessandra's upbringing. While Alessandra's friends were opening presents around the tree on Christmas morning, then sitting down to a rib roast, Alessandra was home alone watching R-rated movies on cable while her mother worked a double. She and her mother opened their Christmas presents on the twenty-sixth with eggs and a tin of osetra caviar and Springsteen singing "Santa Claus Is Coming to Town." On Easter, while Alessandra's friends were going to church and hunting for eggs and slicing into honey-baked ham, Alessandra was watching R-rated movies on cable and eating straight from a bag of jelly beans that her mother bought as a nod to the holiday even though she didn't celebrate Easter at all.

And then there were the men. Every week, Valerie would bring home married men who frequented the Tosca bar while they were in the city on business. These men would arrive after Alessandra went to bed, but she heard them in the shower the next morning while Alessandra's mother ransacked their wallets in the bedroom. Every once in a while, one of the men would stay for breakfast and listen as Valerie played her favorite CD and sang along: *Torn between two lovers, feeling like a fool.*

Alessandra knew better than to follow in her mother's foot-steps but it was the only example she had. When Alessandra was eighteen, she seduced Dr. Andrew Beecham, the father of her best friend, Duffy. After Alessandra and Drew had been sleeping together for a few weeks, Alessandra realized she could cash in on the power she had—the power to tell Duffy and Drew's wife, Mary Lou—and get something valuable in return. Drew was the chair of the romance languages department at Stanford. Alessandra audited a full year of classes—Italian, Spanish, French literature, art history—and then demanded a one-way plane ticket to Rome, which Drew Beecham was only too happy to buy for her.

Where did you come from, Alessandra Powell?

Alessandra answered Michael in her prettiest Italian. *"Poiché la tua domanda cerca un significato profondo, risponderò con parole semplici."* She smiled; she had no intention of translating. "That's Dante."

Michael Bick kissed her tenderly. She was making progress. She stayed the next night and the next.

She made Michael milk-braised pork with hand-rolled gnocchi in sage and butter and a salad of bitter greens. She made coq au vin. She made scrambled eggs the way her mother used to make them for other women's husbands—with double the yolks (double-the-yolk scrambled eggs after a night of whiskey, Valerie used to say, felt a lot like love). Alessandra beat Michael soundly in tennis. (In Ibiza, she had taken lessons with Nadal's first coach.) When they made love, she screamed out in Italian. She didn't complain that they never went anywhere together—not to dinner or coffee, not for walks on the beach or in the state forest, not for drives to Great Point or Sconset. When the guy came to fix the internet, she greeted him in French and told him she was the au pair.

Secretly, Alessandra secured a job at the Hotel Nantucket that would start in June, though she hoped by then Michael would have fallen so deeply in love with her that he would tell Heidi their marriage was over and Alessandra could simply slip into Heidi's place. She would go to Surfside all day while Michael worked at home on his laptop (while he was sleeping, Alessandra had hacked into his computer and learned that he traded petroleum futures and in 2021 had reported $10,793,000 in income), and she would accompany him to Cisco Brewers to hear live music and to his standing Thursday-night reservation at Ventuno. She would become best friends with the Laytons next door; the families were so close that they had a set of keys to each other's house. She would bewitch everyone in Michael's life exactly the way she had bewitched him.

But this didn't quite happen. A few days before Alessandra started work, she overheard Michael on the phone with Heidi and his kids, his voice sweet and upbeat and guileless. "How was the game, Colby, did you hit the ball, did you swing? Hey, buddy, did you see Dustin Johnson sink that putt on the ninth?...I love you, I love you, I love you more, kisses, can't wait to see you all, only two more weeks! I'm getting the boat ready; Coatue, here we come!"

Alessandra felt most affronted by this last bit. She hadn't realized Michael had a boat.

She went to work at the hotel on opening day, disappearing from the house while Michael was on the phone, and she ignored all his calls. Let him wonder. When she walked in the door that evening, he was visibly shaken. "Where were you?" he said.

She narrowed her eyes and tried to read his face. Why did he care? How much did he care? She shrugged. "Out."

A tirade followed; it was the first time she'd seen him angry (other than when the Wi-Fi went down, but that was different), and it interested her. *Worried sick, went driving around looking for you, you just left without a word, the only way I knew you were coming back was your luggage was still here.*

Do you love me? she wondered. She thought the answer might be yes, but it wouldn't be enough.

"I got a job," she said. "Working the front desk at the Hotel Nantucket."

Michael's face turned pill white. "What?"

Alessandra stared him down.

Michael said, "Our...my friend Lizbet Keaton is working there. She's the GM, I heard. Is she the one who hired you?"

"Yes."

Michael nodded slowly, then backed away half a step, as though Alessandra were holding a gun. "You didn't tell her where you were living, did you?"

"Obviously not." Alessandra didn't tell Michael that Lizbet had followed her home. Thankfully, Alessandra had spied her in the bike's mirror before she'd turned into the driveway.

Relief softened his face. "Okay, good. I wouldn't want people to get the wrong idea."

"What you mean," Alessandra said, "is that you wouldn't want people to get the *right* idea. Which is that you're keeping a lover even though you are still fully married. Your wife has no idea you needed space. She thinks you came up here to switch out the storm windows for screens and tackle a 'top secret project' for work, which seems outrageous, but she doesn't question it because she trusts you and she's probably enjoying the time apart—she feeds the kids pizza three nights a week and goes out with her girlfriends to the new wine bar and flirts with the cute bartender and then goes home and curls up with her vibrator." Alessandra stopped to breathe. "You're a liar and a cheat."

Michael cleared his throat. "They're coming up on the eighteenth, so you'll need to go."

"Will I?" Alessandra said.

There was fear in his eyes. *He* was the one who had chosen poorly. "Baby, please."

"I'm not your baby, Michael. I'm a grown woman whom you've treated like a concubine."

"You knew what you were getting into," Michael said. "You can't tell me you didn't understand what this was."

He got everything backward. *He* was the one who didn't understand what this was.

"I'll go quietly the day before your family arrives," Alessandra said. "On one condition."

Alessandra walks from Michael's house to the hotel with a knock-off Louis Vuitton bag in each hand. It's a stylish walk of shame—or it would be if Alessandra felt any shame. What she feels most is regret. Michael Bick is the complete package. He has looks, money, intelligence, humor, and even a basic decency (if you ignore the obvious). He asks questions; he listens to the answers; he's generous and curious and thoughtful. The sex was mind-blowing; Michael is the only man Alessandra ever met who didn't need to learn a thing or two in bed. And they are so compatible. Oh, well. It has been Alessandra's experience that men like Michael Bick get scooped up early, in college or the first years of living as an adult in the city.

She also feels triumphant. In her suede Bruno Magli clutch is a cashier's check for fifty thousand dollars. Michael asked her to name her price and she did so judiciously, unsure of what she could get away with, but now she wonders if she could have asked for double. She won't worry about it. During their first week of sinful bliss, Alessandra watched Michael punch in the passcode to his phone, and later, while he was sleeping, Alessandra copied Heidi Bick's number. She also took pictures of herself in different spots throughout the house—in the pool, weighing herself on Heidi's scale (a trim 105), cooking in the kitchen, even sprawled across the master bed (although they'd never had sex in that room, Michael's one nod to fidelity).

If Alessandra doesn't find another situation, she'll simply text Michael the pictures and ask for more money.

As Heidi Bick is checking things off her packing list in Greenwich—Colby's inhaler, Hayford's putter, her Wüsthof tomato knife—Alessandra will be paying for a 1980 CJ-7 in "mint condition" that she found listed in the *Nantucket Standard* classifieds. The Jeep costs twenty grand; Alessandra will pay cash, then she'll write the bellman Adam a check for twelve grand, which is her share of the summer's rent now that she's moving in with him and Raoul on Hooper Farm Road. She'll throw ten grand at her credit card bills and still have a bit of a financial cushion.

Alessandra is growing weary of seducing men, then extorting them; she would far prefer to find a permanent provider.

She marches up the front steps of the hotel, trying to carry herself like a hotel guest checking in. Except she's wearing her uniform, and Adam says, from his spot behind the lectern, "You look like a high-class hobo."

Alessandra doesn't respond. She pictures Michael frantically cleaning the house, sweeping up every strand of her hair, wiping her fingerprints off the wineglasses, checking the drawers for an errant pair of panties. But will he notice the Chanel eye shadow that Alessandra left in Heidi's makeup drawer in the bathroom?

(Heidi wears Bobbi Brown.) Will he check the shoe tree in Heidi's closet, where Alessandra has left a pair of size 6 crystal-studded René Caovilla stilettos winking coyly among the size 8 Jack Rogers sandals and Tory Burch ballet flats? Will he find the positive pregnancy test that Alessandra tucked into the copy of Jennifer Weiner's *Good in Bed* that sits atop the stack of novels on Heidi Bick's nightstand?

He will not, Alessandra guesses, because men don't pay attention to the way women live, not really. Michael will suffer for this, and for his hubris. He thought he was making a clean (if somewhat costly) getaway.

She wonders if Michael misses her. After handing over the check, he kissed her deeply, and when she pulled away, she saw tears glittering in the corners of his eyes. *Torn between two lovers,* she sang in her head, *feeling like a fool.*

"Raoul says he'll swing by around noon to get your bags," Adam says now.

"Kind of him, thank you," Alessandra says, though she wishes Raoul would come right away so she could avoid the inevitable questions.

Alessandra steps into the lobby and smells the deep roast of the Jamaica Blue Mountain coffee that Edie has percolating (they use a vintage percolator and the guests rave about the flavor). She hears Mandy Patinkin singing a Gershwin song: "They Can't Take That Away from Me."

She's late due to the check, the kiss, the walk with the bags. She likes to arrive before Edie because she feels it gives her the upper hand, and now, when Edie looks up and sees Alessandra and notices the luggage, she looks confused and just a bit superior.

"Good morning, Alessandra," she says. "Taking a trip?" Edie's voice is light and easy despite the fact that Alessandra is always chilly with her.

"Good morning, Edie." It's not that Alessandra doesn't *like* Edie; she does. Edie is smart, self-effacing, and excellent with the Marsh children. (Both Wanda and Louie are terrified of Alessandra.)

But Edie is also young, and the last thing Alessandra wants is for Edie to look up to her. Alessandra doesn't want to lie to Edie about her past or her present, and hence, friendship between them is impossible. Alessandra has to push Edie away.

It's for your own good! Alessandra wants to say, because she can see her brusqueness hurts Edie.

Alessandra drops the bags behind the desk and logs on to her computer.

Lizbet pops out of the back office for what's probably her fourth cup of coffee; she drinks so much caffeine, Alessandra is surprised she doesn't flap her arms and fly away.

Lizbet notices the bags because she notices everything. "What's going on here?" she asks with an arched eyebrow.

Alessandra meets Lizbet's gaze. "My housing fell through, so I'm moving in with Adam and Raoul."

Lizbet moves for the percolator. "What happened to the place on Hulbert?"

Alessandra tries not to care if Lizbet has figured it out. Lizbet can't fire her for what goes on in her personal life, though it might invite scrutiny later on, something Alessandra wants to avoid. She smiles despite the bitter, nearly chemical taste in her mouth. "Oh," she says, "that was just temporary."

Chad has been assigned a cleaning partner named Bibi Evans who treats every room like it's a crime scene. This might be because Bibi aspires to be a forensic scientist, or it might be because Bibi is what Chad's mother would call a "nosy parker," or it might be because Bibi is a thief. Chad doesn't like thinking this last thing, but that's what his gut tells him, because Bibi touches every single item in any room that might be worth stealing. She touches the things that Ms. English has expressly asked them *not* to touch, such as watches, jewelry, cash, and pills.

They've been working together for two weeks when Bibi lifts a diamond tennis bracelet out of a travel jewelry case and *tries it on*. Chad is freaked out (and also somewhat impressed) at Bibi's moxie; she doesn't seem to be intimidated by Ms. English or the rules. Bibi holds her hand out so that the diamonds catch the sunlight coming in through the picture window overlooking Easton Street. "I was meant for the finer things."

"You should probably put that back," Chad says.

"You're such a *rule follower*." She says this like she's calling him a pedophile.

It would be easy for Chad to shock Bibi with the ways that he's broken the rules, but it's nothing to be proud of. "The guest could walk in any second, Bibi," he says. "Or Ms. English."

Bibi waves her arm around as though showing off the bracelet to a roomful of admirers. It looks wrong on her pale, knobby wrist. Bibi wears heavy black eyeliner and has a tattoo of a skull on the back of her neck, which Chad noticed when Ms. English insisted that Bibi gather her stringy dark hair into a ponytail. She's nothing like the girls Chad went to high school or college with; Chad understands that she's from a different "socioeconomic class." Bibi is the mother of a nine-month-old girl, Smoky (that's her actual name; it's not short for anything). She told Chad that she took this "crappy job" because she wants to go to college, study forensics, and join the homicide unit of the Massachusetts State Police so that she can give Smoky a better life than the one she had growing up. Bibi's life involved a drunk for a mother (Chad can commiserate with her there, though he's not sure his own mother and Bibi's mother have much else in common). Bibi often lamented that paying for child care and the ferry tickets from the Cape took more than half her paycheck. Chad made what he hoped sounded like sympathetic noises. He told her the baby was cute.

"You're a complete squid, Long Shot," Bibi said that first day. "Long Shot" was the nickname Ms. English had given him and he's secretly pleased because, on Nantucket, any name is better than Chad. "But I'd rather be paired with you than with those other bitches."

She meant Octavia and Neves. They speak Portuguese and wear thick gold crosses around their necks. Ms. English refers to Octavia and Neves as the A-team and Chad and Bibi as the B-team, which is probably not a random designation. This might be what fuels Bibi's dislike of the other girls (Chad doesn't care; he knows he belongs on the B-team), although Bibi's vitriol is so intense that Chad wonders if the sisters are mean to Bibi on the ferry. (He can't imagine this.) By her own admission, Bibi hates people. It's the one thing, she says, that brings her joy.

Chad announces that he'll clean the bathroom and deal with the floral bouquets if Bibi wants to vacuum and get started on the bed. She grunts in the affirmative, though Chad was hoping for a thank-you, since he's taking the more onerous tasks. The flowers are a surprisingly tedious job—he has to wipe up the blue hydrangea dust, trim the stamens of the lilies because pollen stains everything a bloody rust color, and change the smelly brown water in the vase. But the flowers are a picnic compared to cleaning the bathroom. In the two weeks that Chad has been working at the hotel, he's dealt with bloody pads and tampons in the trash (he appreciates anew that he and his sister never had to share a bathroom), and he cleaned up the puke of some bachelor-party dude who didn't make it anywhere close to the toilet bowl. Only slightly less repulsive are the globs of toothpaste and stray hairs he has to scrub from the sink.

By dealing with the flowers and the bathroom, he achieves the dual purpose of punishing himself and sucking up to Bibi. Her approval matters, even though she's not pretty and not sophisticated and not particularly well educated; despite her claim that she is "meant for the finer things," everything about her demeanor suggests otherwise. She's a twenty-one-year-old single mother (she hasn't mentioned the father of the baby and Chad isn't brave enough to ask), and Chad is both in awe of and afraid of her.

When Chad finishes scrubbing the shower and the tub—he does the tub conscientiously even though it's clear it hasn't been used—he pokes his head into the bedroom. The bed has been stripped and remade, the pillows artfully arranged; Bibi always does a really good job with the beds. Chad doesn't see Bibi, but instead of calling her name, he tiptoes around. He finds her in the walk-in closet, sifting through a suitcase. She holds up a belt first, then an amethyst silk negligée. He notices she still has the tennis bracelet on her wrist.

"Bibi?" he says.

She jumps. "Jeez, Long Shot, you scared me. What the hell?"

"What are you doing?" he asks. "You know we're not supposed to go through personal stuff. And you need to take that bracelet off."

"Who are you, the cleaning police?"

"I just don't want you to get in trouble."

"Why would I get in trouble? I'm just looking around. I'm not going to *take* anything. You probably think I'm a thief because I'm not rich like you, Mr. Eel Point Road. Mr. Range Rover."

Chad blinks. He's not sure how Bibi discovered what he drives or where he lives. He's been careful to present himself as a normalish summer kid. He parks way up on Cliff Road and told her only that he lived on a "dirt road, out of town."

"I don't think you're a thief, Bibi," he says. He's tempted in that moment to offer her part of this week's paycheck because he knows she has to buy things like diapers and formula, but he's afraid she'll find it patronizing. "Do you want me to do the vacuuming?"

The next morning, Ms. English sends Octavia and Neves to clean suite 114—Chad is grateful they're doing it, because being around Doug the pit bull makes him uncomfortable—but instead of giving Chad and Bibi a roster of rooms and sending them out too, Ms. English closes her office door and turns to them.

"The guests in room one oh five reported something missing," she says. "A black-and-gold Fendi scarf."

Chad closes his eyes. Room 105 was the last room they cleaned yesterday; it was a checkout. In room 105, Bibi had been suspiciously on task and Chad thought this was because the guests had left a forty-dollar tip, which Chad told Bibi she could take. Bibi had asked if he wanted to go down to the service kitchen to replenish the items that went in the minibar—the wine, the Cisco beers, the bluefish pâté and crackers—which was the best job of all. The service kitchen was adjacent to the Blue Bar kitchen, where Beatriz was usually pulling a tray out of the oven—gougères or homemade pigs in a blanket or the pretzel bread—and she always offered some of whatever it was to the cleaning staff. Yesterday afternoon, Chad hit the jackpot because Beatriz was prepping lobster-roll sliders on homemade milk buns. Chad had eaten lobster growing up the way other kids ate peanut butter and jelly but he had never eaten anything like this slider before. The outside of the milk bun was crisply toasted while the inside was fragrant and pillowy; the lobster meat had been mixed with lemon zest, herbs, crunchy pieces of celery, and just enough tangy mayo. The lobster slider was so...*elevated* that Chad went back to room 105 feeling inspired. He wanted to do his job as well as Beatriz did hers. He wanted to clean the *hell* out of room 105!

But when he returned, the room was finished and Bibi was gone. Chad peered out the window to see Bibi heading down North Beach Street toward the ferry with her backpack slung over her shoulder. He was sorry she'd left—he'd brought a slider up for her—but also relieved that he'd survived another day with her.

"Did either of you see a black-and-gold scarf?" Ms. English asks. "Because Mrs. Daley is sure she left one behind. She sent a picture of herself wearing it at Ventuno and she says it's not in her luggage. Did you find it and put it in the lost and found?" Ms. English pauses. "Did you perhaps *mean* to put it in the lost and found and forget to?"

She's giving Bibi a way out, Chad thinks. Because Bibi definitely lifted that scarf.

"I didn't see any scarves," Bibi says in a clear, steady voice that sounds so genuine, Chad believes her. "Did you, Long Shot?"

"No," he says. "And we checked all the drawers like we were supposed to."

"Yes, I double-checked as well," Ms. English says. She studies their faces. Ms. English is a handsome woman who has never been anything but nice to Chad; even when she made him fold a hand towel for the sixtieth time, he felt like she was doing it for his own good. She has high standards and a dignity that Chad respects. He does *not* want to disappoint her.

"Did you look in the laundry?" Bibi asks. "Maybe Mr. and Mrs. Daley were using the scarf in bed—you know, to tie each other up—and it got mixed in with the sheets."

"Of course I've checked the laundry," Ms. English says. She clears her throat. "I understand how tempting it is when you see something you covet and you think the guest has so many things that she might not miss something like a scarf..."

"It sounds like you're accusing us of taking it," Bibi says. "Which is not only insulting, it's absurd. Chadwick has family money, plus a dude would have no use for a woman's scarf. And I would never take it, because scarves like that are for boomers. Sorry, for older women. Plus I wouldn't be able to tell a Fendi scarf from a Walmart scarf."

That's a lie, Chad thinks. Bibi *loves* designer stuff. She makes a game of identifying the designers of bags, belts, and shoes without checking the labels—Chloé, Balenciaga, Louboutin—and she's always right.

Bibi says, "Besides, I would never steal from a guest. I have a baby at home. I'm a *mother.*" She pauses. "Did you ask Octavia and Neves if *they've* seen it?"

Chad lowers his gaze to the floor. He can't believe she's going there.

"The scarf was missing from room one oh five," Ms. English says. "That was your room to clean."

"But they each have a master key," Bibi says. "It's not impossible that they took it and tried to make it look like it was us. They have some kind of weird grudge against me that you should be aware of."

Ms. English is quiet. Chad is quiet. Bibi isn't speaking but there's a lot of disruption emanating from her. Or maybe Chad is projecting.

"I'll let Mrs. Daley know that we haven't found it but that we'll keep looking," Ms. English says. "Maybe it's in Mr. Daley's luggage or perhaps she took it off while she was out and left it somewhere. But I do hope nothing else goes missing."

Chad and Bibi take their cart up to room 307 in silence. Bibi doesn't touch anything in the room, and she offers to clean the bathroom and do the flowers, which, Chad realizes, is as close to an admission of guilt as he's going to get.

9. The Cobblestone Telegraph

The summer season is under way on the island and most of us are too busy with our own lives—tracking down the window washer, mulching our gardens, pulling our beach chairs out of storage—to pay attention to the happenings at the Hotel Nantucket. But every once in a while, we'll drive past and see Zeke English standing on the sidewalk in front of the hotel with a pit bull on a leash sniffing the dandelions, and we'll wonder how things are going.

Blond Sharon is having dinner at the Deck one evening when JJ O'Malley himself pops out to say hello. Blond Sharon does the intrepid thing and asks if he's heard how Lizbet likes her new job.

"No, I haven't," JJ says. "We don't speak."

"Well, I'm sure she's busy," Blond Sharon says. "Have you eaten at the Blue Bar yet? Everyone's raving about it. They have a copper disco ball that drops—"

"Out of the ceiling at nine o'clock," JJ says. "Yes, I know. But from what I've heard, you can't have a proper dinner there, right? He isn't serving a chop or a rib eye or even a pan roast."

"Right," Blond Sharon says. "It's more like great cocktail-party food, heavy apps that you can share, and then after you've finished grazing, someone comes around with shot glasses of whipped cream in flavors like Kahlúa and passion fruit. It's called the whipped cream concierge! Have you ever heard of anything so fabulous? And then everyone starts dancing. We went last week and, honestly, I've never had more fun in my life."

JJ O'Malley squares up to his full height and gazes across the creeks, perhaps to remind Blond Sharon that although the Deck doesn't have a *whipped cream concierge,* it does have a magnificent view. "The reviews of the hotel on TravelTattler have been underwhelming," he says.

"Oh," Blond Sharon says. "Have you been checking?"

Officer Dixon gets a call at four o'clock in the afternoon about a man asleep in his car at Dionis Beach.

"So what?" Dixon says to Sheila in dispatch.

"I guess he's been sleeping in his car in the parking lot the past three days," Sheila says. "Some mommy noticed him and thinks he's a potential predator."

Dixon takes a breath. A man sleeping in his car is what passes for crime on Nantucket; he supposes he should be glad. He climbs into his cruiser.

When he arrives at Dionis, he sees the man and the car in question—some guy in his early fifties in a 2010 Honda Pilot with Connecticut plates and a WHAT WOULD JIM CALHOUN DO? bumper sticker. The back window sports a decal that says PARENT OF AN AVON MIDDLE SCHOOL HONOR STUDENT.

Threatening stuff. Dixon wonders if he'll need to call for backup.

He approaches the open car window and sees the guy in the driver's seat, head slumped back, snoring away. He's wearing a white polo shirt and swim trunks; his bifocals have slid down to the end of his nose, and there's a copy of Lee Child's *Blue Moon* splayed open in the console next to an open Red Bull. Dixon backs away because he feels like he's intruding on the guy in his bedroom— and then he notices the open shaving kit on the passenger seat and a hand towel drying on the dashboard. A peek into the back seat reveals a gaping suitcase.

Is this guy...Dixon glances over at the public bathrooms. Dionis is the only beach on Nantucket that has showers. Is this guy *living* in his car?

"Excuse me, sir," Dixon says, jostling the guy's shoulder. "May I see your license and registration, please?"

Richard Decameron, age fifty-four, of Avon, Connecticut, here on the island to work for the summer at the Hotel Nantucket.

"So you're not...living in this car?" Dixon asks. "Because that's what it looks like."

Decameron tries to laugh this off, but it isn't quite convincing. "No, no, I live at the hotel."

"Why are you sleeping here in the parking lot? We've had reports that you've been here the past three days."

"I'm enjoying the beach," Decameron says. "I take an early swim, get a shower, read my book, and sometimes I conk out." He offers Dixon a friendly smile. "Is that against the law?"

He's "enjoying the beach" by sleeping in the parking lot? Something doesn't add up. "What's your position at the hotel?" Dixon asks.

"I work the front desk," Decameron says.

Dixon nods. Nothing about this guy screams predator or even vagrant. He seems like a regular guy—a Huskies basketball fan, the father of an honor student.

"So tell me something," Dixon says. "Have you seen the ghost?"

"Not yet," Decameron says. "She's playing hard to get."

Dixon chuckles and slaps the roof of the car. "All right, I'm not going to issue a ticket. Tomorrow, though, you'd better find a different beach."

"Will do, Officer," Decameron says. "Thank you."

* * *

Lyric Layton is in her kitchen at seven a.m. making a beet-and-blueberry smoothie after doing yoga on her private beach when she hears a light rapping on her front door. Anne Boleyn, Lyric's chocolate British shorthair, rises and places her paws on Lyric's shin, which is something she does only when she's anxious. Lyric scoops up the cat and goes to see who on earth is knocking at this hour.

It's Heidi Bick from next door. The Laytons and the Bicks have plans to go to Galley Beach for dinner that night. Lyric wonders if Heidi has somehow heard her news; Lyric was planning on telling Heidi at dinner if Heidi didn't guess when Lyric ordered sparkling water instead of champagne. But then she sees the stricken look on Heidi's face.

"Are you the only one up?" Heidi whispers. "I need to talk."

"Yes, of course," Lyric says. Her husband, Ari, and the three boys would sleep until noon every day of the summer if she'd let them. "Come on in."

Lyric leads Heidi into the kitchen, offers her a smoothie—no, thank you, she can't manage any—and then Lyric opens the slider so they can sit out on the deck. The rising sun spangles the water of Nantucket Sound; the early-morning ferry is gliding past Brant Point Light and out of the harbor.

"I think Michael is having an affair," Heidi says. She gives a strangled little laugh. "I can't believe I just said those words. I sound like someone on Netflix. I mean, it's *Michael.* We're Michael and Heidi *Bick.* This isn't supposed to happen."

Well, well, well, Lyric thinks. "Whoa, honey, start at the beginning. What gives you this idea?"

"I'm so stupid!" Heidi says. "Michael has been living up here since April. He told me he and his coworker Rafe were making moves to splinter off and start their own company. He chose to work remotely so he had the necessary privacy. Did I ask any questions? No! I took him at his word—and I was happy for some time to myself. Meanwhile, he was up here with someone else!"

To anyone other than Lyric Layton, this news about Michael might have come as a jaw-dropping surprise. Michael and Heidi Bick were widely considered to be "the perfect couple"—everyone said it here on Nantucket and back in Greenwich as well. But Lyric has gotten certain...vibes from Michael. Last summer when Lyric and Ari and Michael and Heidi were at dinner at the Deck, Lyric caught Michael staring at her from across the table. She thought she was imagining it—a lot of rosé had been consumed—but then he touched her leg with his foot. Lyric had quickly tucked her legs under her chair. She said nothing to Ari or to Heidi because she was sure Michael was just being a naughty drunk. Lyric considers herself an excellent friend—she remembers birthdays, she takes extra carpool shifts, she polishes other queens' crowns—so she would never, *ever* entertain the notion of an affair with Michael. But...if she's painfully honest, she would admit that there have been times when she was practicing yoga on the beach and wondered if Michael Bick was in his master bathroom, fresh out of the shower, watching her from the window.

Lyric arranges her facial expression into one of both skepticism and concern. "Oh, Heidi, I doubt that."

"So you haven't heard any rumors about Michael running around the island with some other woman?" Heidi presses the heels of her palms into her eye sockets. "I had this horrible idea that everyone knew but me and everyone was talking about it..."

"I've heard nothing," Lyric says. "And I had lunch with Blond Sharon at the Field and Oar Club yesterday. She didn't say a word. What makes you *think* this?"

Heidi pulls a Chanel eye shadow out of the pocket of her jeans jacket. It's a half-used cream shadow in Pourpre Brun. "This was in my makeup drawer."

Lyric takes the eye shadow. "Not your color," she says. She's trying to make a joke, but inside, Lyric is shrieking. It's not *Heidi's* color, but it is *Lyric's* color—and Lyric wears only Chanel eye shadow, as Heidi well knows. Lyric wonders if Heidi is accusing Lyric of having an affair with Michael. This is getting extremely sticky. Has Michael been sleeping with someone who wears Chanel eye shadow in one of Lyric's go-to shades? He must be. Why else would the shadow be in Heidi's makeup drawer? Lyric feels a little jealous herself—which is insane, of course. She's happily married and pregnant with her fourth child. "Have you asked Michael about it?" Lyric says.

"No," Heidi says. "I'm going to wait and see if I find anything else."

Lyric agrees this is a good idea. It's probably nothing; maybe it was the cleaning lady's (this makes no sense) or it belongs to Colby, Heidi's daughter (she's only eleven, but kids are precocious these days). She says she's certain there's a reasonable explanation. Lyric shepherds Heidi to the door in something of a rush because she feels morning sickness wash over her (the beet-and-blueberry smoothie, ick; what had made her think that would be a good combo?). "Try to relax, Michael loves you, see you tonight at dinner." Lyric might not tell Heidi she's pregnant tonight, because how awful to share happy news when her friend is suffering.

Lyric shuts the door behind Heidi and runs down the hall to the bathroom, where she vomits up the smoothie. After rinsing her mouth, she goes hunting for her own Chanel cream eye shadow in Pourpre Brun.

The funny thing is, she can't find it.

Jasper Monroe of Fisher Island, Florida, wakes up in suite 115 of the Hotel Nantucket to a text from his mother: Where are you??? Did you not come home last night??? You know the rules, Jasper!!!

Jasper groans and rolls over. He kisses Winston on the shoulder and says, "I have to get out of here, man. My mom is kerking."

"Your *mom?*" Winston says.

"Yeah," Jasper says. He feels like he's twelve years old, and he senses that Winston, who was Jasper's teaching assistant at Trinity, wants to remind him that he's twenty-two, a grown man, and that he can stay out all night if he wants. But the fact remains that Jasper lives under his parents' roof and he did break a house rule by not telling his mother that he'd be out all night, and beyond that, his parents don't know he's gay. Nobody does.

Jasper puts on his Nantucket Reds and his polo, both rumpled and beer-soaked after a late night at the Chicken Box. He decides to get his mother half a dozen of the infamous morning buns from Wicked Island Bakery as an apology.

"Catch you later, man," Jasper says.

"When?" Winston asks.

Jasper isn't sure. Winston came to Nantucket specifically to see Jasper, but Jasper has to be careful. "I'll snap."

Winston gets out of bed to see Jasper out, so he can't be that mad. They do some pretty heavy-duty kissing in the doorway.

"Come back to bed," Winston murmurs into Jasper's mouth.

Jasper is actually considering it—his mom isn't going to be any madder in an hour than she is now—but then he hears a rattling and turns to see the housekeeping cart rounding the corner, and pushing that cart is...Chad Winslow.

What? Chad is wearing khakis and a blue polo, and he's with some beaten-down-looking chick who smirks at Jasper and shirtless Winston and says, "You gentlemen ready for service?"

"Jasper?" Chad says.

Jasper feels like a coyote with his leg in a trap. "Chad? Are you...*working* here, man?" Jasper and his buddies Eric and Bryce have all been wondering what's up with Chad, but him having a *job* never crossed their minds. A job cleaning rooms at a *hotel?* It makes no sense.

Chad shrugs and casts his eyes over Jasper's shoulder at Winston. "Yeah, I'm a maid," Chad says. "What are you doing here?"

I'm a maid. It must be a joke, right? Except Jasper can tell it isn't and Chad doesn't seem the least bit embarrassed. It's like Winston is always saying: There is nothing shameful about who we really are.

"Stayed over with my boyfriend, Winston," Jasper says. And just like that, he's out. He grins. He can't believe how easy that was.

Chad nods. "Cool. Nice to meet you, Winston."

"Nice to meet you," Winston says.

"Nice, nice, nice," the chick with Chad says. "So, are you ready for service or what?"

Nancy Twine passes around the offering basket at the Summer Street Church. She tries not to notice how much a person gives; three dollars for some is as much of a sacrifice as thirty dollars for others. But it does catch her attention when Magda English drops several folded hundred-dollar bills into the basket. (*Five* hundred-dollar bills, Nancy would come to find out when she counts the money after the service.)

Now, where does Magda English, who moved here back in September to care for her poor bereaved brother, William, and her nephew Ezekiel and who is working as head of housekeeping at the haunted hotel on the other side of town, come up with that kind of money? Nancy can't begin to guess.

10. Last Friday of the Month: June

Lizbet, Edie, Adam, and Alessandra are crowded into Lizbet's office at 11:55 a.m. on June 24 so they can refresh their Instagram feeds right at noon.

Adam is the first one to see Shelly Carpenter's post. "It's the Isthmus in New York City. Four keys."

"Kind of boring?" Alessandra says. "Although she hasn't done New York in a while."

"She reviewed the William Vale in March of last year," Edie says.

"It's scary that you know that," Adam says. He swipes through the pictures while Lizbet, Edie, and Alessandra click on the link. Frankly, Lizbet is relieved that the Hotel Nantucket wasn't chosen; they're nowhere near ready.

Hotel Confidential by Shelly Carpenter

June 24, 2022

The Isthmus Hotel, New York, New York—4 KEYS 🔑

Hello again, friends!

The Isthmus Hotel chain has been synonymous with luxury and sophisticated service since the flagship opened in Panama City in 1904 to cater to visitors coming to view the man-made wonder of the canal. The Manhattan outpost, located on the very desirable southeast corner of Fifty-Fifth and Fifth, has long been a top choice for discerning travelers, especially those from Central and South America, who appreciate the bilingual staff.

The hotel underwent a soup-to-nuts renovation in 2019 with all rooms given a much-needed makeover. They've opted for a clean, modern look—the rooms feature a lot of ivory and pearl gray and may be the teensiest bit generic. The lights of each room are all on a master panel inside the door and offer three choices: Festival (every light in the room on), Romance (low mood lighting), and Nighty-Night (every light in the room off). I tried to figure out how to beat the system and turn some lights off and some on (the one next to my bed, for example). It seemingly can't be done without a degree in electrical engineering.

I wanted to check the concierge's knowledge of the area, so I requested the name of a salon where I could get an inexpensive pedicure within ten blocks on a Sunday. The concierge found me a place right away, but when I went to write down the address on the notepad next to the phone, I found the hotel pen was dry. Readers of this column may feel this is a tiny detail—and make no mistake, it is—but if a hotel is providing an amenity such as a pen, it should work.

The other aspects of my stay at the Isthmus were top-notch. The bedding was delicious, the comforter as fluffy as a mound of whipped cream; the toiletries in the sleek marble-and-chrome bathroom (which was massive by New York standards) were scented with sandalwood, and the water pressure in the shower was strong but not painful. My bags were delivered only two minutes after I arrived, and when ice was requested, it came within five minutes. Room service exceeded all expectations. The Isthmus in-room-dining menu includes some Panamanian flair with the additions of sancocho de gallina and chicheme, both of which I ordered and both of which were better and more reasonably priced than standard room-service fare.

Overall, I award the Isthmus Hotel in New York a solid four keys with a plea to any hoteliers reading this review: Put an individual switch on each lamp, one that's easy to find and preferably with a dimmer. Thank you!

Stay well, friends. And do good.

—SC

"Our lights all have individual switches, and the table and floor lamps have dimmers!" Edie says.

"I can't believe she complained about the *pens*," Adam says. "I would never have thought to check the pens."

"Ms. English has the staff check every pen," Alessandra says.

"Yes," Lizbet says. The Hotel Nantucket pens are Uni-Ball Jetstream—the best—and they write smooth and dark. She's proud of their pen game. But the fact remains that no detail escapes Shelly Carpenter's notice. Their lighting and pens are up to snuff, but there might be a dozen other things Shelly could find fault with.

When—if—she comes.

11. The Blue Book

June 27, 2022
From: Xavier Darling (xd@darlingent.co.uk)
To: Employees of the Hotel Nantucket

Good morning, staff! I'm pleased to finally be able to an-
nounce a winner of the weekly bonus that I promised you all
back on opening day. The winner for the week of June 20 was
front-desk manager Alessandra Powell. Alessandra received
a glowing review from one of our guests on TravelTattler for her
outstanding customer service. Congratulations, Alessandra!
Keep up the good work!

XD

As they enter the final week of June, hotel operations lose their
new-shoe stiffness and start to feel fluid and organic. (Speaking of
shoes, Lizbet has traded in her stilettos for wedges, an idea she
stole from Alessandra, and she's far more comfortable.) There was
one complaint on TravelTattler, about a missing Fendi scarf, that
did some damage—a mystery that remains unsolved, according to
Magda—but the rest of the reviews have been positive and Xavier
finally relented and granted the first thousand-dollar bonus, to

Alessandra because some anonymous reviewer raved about her. (If Lizbet had to guess, she would say it was Mr. Brownlee from room 309; he made no secret of the fact that he found Alessandra to be the most beautiful creature he'd ever laid eyes on.) Lizbet would rather have seen the bonus go to anyone else—Raoul, for example, the unsung hero of the evening bell desk, or Sweet Edie—but it went to Alessandra and no one has expressed any resentment. They're probably intimidated.

Lizbet's outlook has improved since Richie started working nights. Lizbet now leaves the hotel at five thirty, fits in a run or a ride on her Peloton, makes herself some dinner (she's so tired, she can usually only manage a tuna fish sandwich or ramen noodles), then takes her laptop to bed with the intention of catching up on current events or bingeing a show so that she has something to chat with the guests about, but most nights, she falls asleep within five minutes of getting in bed.

Lizbet hasn't been out anywhere socially since she and JJ broke up, and now that she's finally ready, invitations are lacking. She'd thought that she and Heidi Bick had semi-confirmed plans on the eighteenth, but when Lizbet texted to definitively confirm, Heidi canceled. She said she needed "couple time" with Michael. Being ditched for someone else's couple time made Lizbet feel like a lonesome loser. Lizbet has other friends, but unfortunately, they're all tethered in one way or another to the Deck, and Lizbet doesn't feel she can reach out lest it seem like she's poaching from JJ's territory or, worse still, desperate. Again, she's hurt that Goose and Wavy and Peyton all seem to have abandoned her or "chosen" JJ like they're children in a divorce. Not only does Lizbet miss them but she would like to know how things are going without her. Who has JJ put on the reservation book? Probably Peyton—she's the most capable and would have been Lizbet's choice if anyone had asked, which of course no one did.

It's bright and early on the first of July—there's something fresh and optimistic about the first of the month, and Lizbet has high hopes for occupancy at the hotel picking up. Edie pokes her head into Lizbet's office and says, "There's a woman out front who would like to speak with you."

Lizbet jumps to her feet, ever mindful that Shelly Carpenter could appear at any moment. It's the Fourth of July week, which is traditionally crazy busy, and it's common knowledge that Shelly Carpenter tends to show up at hotels during stressful or extraordinary times.

But Lizbet's spirits flag when she sees it's Mrs. Amesbury. There is no universe where Mrs. Amesbury is actually Shelly Carpenter. Mrs. Amesbury came to complain to Lizbet the day before because cute Mrs. Damiani was breastfeeding her infant son in the lobby and Mrs. Amesbury found it distasteful.

"How can I help you, Mrs. Amesbury?" Lizbet asks. It nearly hurts, but Lizbet manages to smile. Mr. Amesbury—he's the kind of husband who carries his wife's handbag—is standing behind Mrs. Amesbury just as he was yesterday when Mrs. Amesbury complained about the breastfeeding.

Mrs. Amesbury holds out the Blue Book; it's open to the restaurant section. "This has a glaring error."

"Error?" Lizbet says, growing warm with panic. The Blue Book is her pet project. She double-checked all addresses, phone numbers, hours of operation, websites, and other pertinent details such as dress code, price range, and reservation protocol. She's very proud of the book and has actually considered submitting it to a mainstream publisher. The world needs a Nantucket guidebook written by an island insider. "What kind of error?"

"The Deck isn't in here!" Mrs. Amesbury says. "It's the most important and successful restaurant on the entire island and you *forgot* to include it!"

Lizbet blinks. She can't pretend to feel surprised, because she knew this moment would come. Lizbet didn't *forget* the Deck; she purposely left it out. It might seem like a startling omission, but Lizbet doesn't care. There was no way she was putting JJ's restaurant in the Blue Book.

Lizbet says, "I'm aware it's not included, Mrs. Amesbury. I wanted to showcase the island's *other* restaurants, ones you might not be familiar with. Have you ever eaten at Or, The Whale? What about Straight Wharf?"

"We'd like to eat at the Deck," Mrs. Amesbury says. "On the evening of the Fourth."

"Ah," Lizbet says. The Deck *is* magical on the Fourth of July. Not only does JJ throw down a pig roast with family-style sides of baked beans, pickled chowchow, corn bread, and potato salad, but guests can enjoy a view of the fireworks across the harbor. Last year, Lizbet hired a bluegrass band and people danced until midnight. "The Deck probably sold out for that evening weeks ago."

"I'd like you to check for me, please," Mrs. Amesbury says.

"Have you ever eaten at the Tap Room?" Lizbet lowers her voice. "They have a secret Big Mac that's not on the menu."

"I've never eaten a Big Mac in my life," Mrs. Amesbury says. "We'd like to go to the Deck."

Lizbet nods robotically. "Their phone lines open at three. I'll have Edie call."

"I'd prefer *you* to call," Mrs. Amesbury says. "You're the general manager; you'll have the most clout. If it's as difficult to get a reservation as you claim, we'll need every advantage."

Ha-ha-ha-ha! Lizbet thinks. "I'd be happy to call myself, Mrs. Amesbury. I'll call at three o'clock on the nose."

But at three o'clock on the nose, Lizbet is up on the fourth floor testing out the ladder that leads to the hotel's widow's walk. The walk is quite large, probably big enough to hold thirty people, and Lizbet is thinking of offering a viewing platform to guests for the fireworks. Something to rival the Deck?

The ladder is rickety and steep. Lizbet manages to climb up, but not without effort. This won't work for the Fourth, but even so, she unhooks the hatch door and pulls herself up so she can take in the dazzling panorama. Lizbet can see all the way down to the yellow, green, and blue umbrellas of the Beach Club; she can see Brant Point Light and the streets of town in a neat four-block grid.

"What are you doing?"

Lizbet gasps. Wanda, holding her notebook and pencil, is standing at the bottom of the ladder.

"What are *you* doing?" Lizbet asks. "I thought we made it clear this floor is off-limits."

Wanda nods seriously. "I know. But this is where the ghost lives."

Lizbet nearly snaps, *There is no ghost, why isn't your mother keeping a closer eye on you? This hotel isn't your playhouse,* but Wanda, with her white-blond hair and her thick glasses, is too adorable to scold. She's wearing a red gingham dress with strawberries embroidered on the rickrack in front. Other eight-year-old girls, Lizbet suspects, are waltzing around in cutoffs and crop tops, checking their Instagram accounts.

Lizbet closes the trapdoor tight and takes Wanda by the hand. "Let's go."

When they reach the desk, Mrs. Amesbury is waiting. "Did you secure my reservation at the Deck?"

Lizbet considers saying, *Yes, I called at three and they're booked solid.* But she can't bring herself to lie. "I'm so sorry, Mrs. Amesbury, I completely spaced about it. I'll call now."

Mrs. Amesbury nods with her lips pressed tight, as though she expected this kind of dropped ball. "I'll wait."

What can Lizbet do but pick up the phone and call the Deck?

"Good afternoon, the Deck." The female voice that answers is familiar, but it's not Peyton. Lizbet runs through her former staff, trying to put a name to the voice. Or maybe JJ hired someone new?

"Good afternoon, this is Lizbet Keaton calling from the Hotel Nantucket?" She waits for a response but is met with silence. "We have a party of two here at the hotel who would like a reservation on Monday evening at"—Lizbet looks at Mrs. Amesbury, who holds up seven fingers—"seven o'clock." There's no way Mrs. Amesbury is going to get seven. Five thirty or nine thirty maybe, *maybe,* if there's been a last-minute cancellation.

"By Monday, you mean the Fourth?" the voice says.

"Yes, the Fourth of July. At seven o'clock. For two people." Lizbet might as well be asking for the moon to be shot out of the sky or for the ocean to be dyed purple.

"Very good," the voice says. "What's the name?"

Lizbet is rendered temporarily speechless. Is it possible Mrs. Amesbury *will* get a seven o'clock reservation on the Fourth of July? Have things at the Deck gotten so bad that they have a table *available?* Lizbet isn't sure how to feel about this. She wants to gloat—the restaurant is failing without her—but she also feels sad that the place she invested so much energy in has fallen like a sloppy Jenga tower.

"Amesbury," she says. "And again, they're staying with us here at the Hotel Nantucket."

Mrs. Amesbury flashes Lizbet a smug smile. Lizbet can hear the words *I told you so.*

"Please let the Amesburys know they're number fifty-seven on the wait list for that date and time. Should a table become available, we'll let you know."

"Ah," Lizbet says. She'll be able to volley the *I told you so* right back to Mrs. Amesbury, but she's not happy about it. "We'll keep our fingers crossed, I guess. Thank you so much."

"Anything for you, Lizbet," the voice says.

"I'm sorry, I know I recognize your voice, but I can't quite place it," Lizbet says. "Who is this?"

There's a beat of silence before the voice speaks again. "It's Christina."

Lizbet hangs up and somehow finds the ability to smile at Mrs. Amesbury. "You're number fifty-seven on the wait list," she says. "Shall we try the Tap Room?"

This is why nobody from the Deck has reached out, Lizbet thinks. They didn't want to tell her, or they assumed she already knew: Christina is managing the front of the house. Christina is the new Lizbet.

When Lizbet gets off work, she heads straight into the Blue Bar like a woman possessed. Service for the evening has just begun, so the place has the feel of a Broadway show before the curtain lifts. The copper dome lights over the bar gleam; the stools are perfectly aligned and set at an inviting angle: *Come sit on me!* The stereo is playing Tony Bennett singing "The Best Is Yet to Come." Lizbet has wanted to stop in for a cocktail since day one, but she was too tired and too embarrassed about being alone. But tonight, she needs a drink and a chance to quietly process JJ's newest betrayal.

The bartender appears, her blue button-down pressed, cuffs turned back neatly at the wrists. She grins. "Hey, Lizbet."

"Hey, Petey," Lizbet says. Patricia "Petey" Casstevens is a Nantucket superstar; for ten years, she lit up the front bar at Cru. She's in her fifties, weighs a hundred pounds with a pocketful of change, and she's fiercely loyal to all Nantucket locals.

"I'll have the Heartbroken, please," Lizbet says.

Petey furrows her brow. "The... oh, you mean the Heartbreaker? The drink Chef named for you?"

That's right—Lizbet is the breaker, not the broken. This is as good an affirmation as any; she'll write it in her phone. "He told you that?"

"It's the best drink on the menu." Petey goes about mixing the various juices like an alchemist and she includes an eye-popping pour of Belvedere vodka. "Strong drink for a strong woman," she says. "Word on the cobblestones is the Deck's not half as good without you there." This is nice to hear, though Lizbet suspects Petey is fluffing her.

Lizbet revisits the last time she saw JJ, when he'd gotten down on one knee in the crushed shells of the parking lot and, unless she's misremembering, *proposed.* Now, only three and a half weeks later, Christina is back, swirling her oaky chardonnays in JJ's emotional life. JJ is such a skunk. Such a disingenuous jerk. Why doesn't knowing this make the hurt go away? Why does finding out that Christina is now working—and, who is she kidding, *sleeping*—with JJ make him seem more desirable? It's a false construct, Lizbet tells herself. We all want what we can't have.

But this doesn't make her feel any better.

Anything for you, Lizbet, Christina said while she stuck Mrs. Amesbury in reservation Siberia.

Petey slides the Heartbreaker across the bar. Its deep red-orange color is even more mesmerizing than Lizbet remembers and she knows she should savor every sip—but she downs it in three long swallows. JJ and Christina are not only living rent-free in Lizbet's head, they've moved in their new Crate and Barrel furniture. How does she evict them? With all the advances in medicine and technology, why has someone not created a pill that cures heartbreak? Emotional penicillin. Why has someone not invented software that will sweep all traces of your ex out of your brain or an app that eliminates unrequited love?

"I'm going to tell Chef you're here," Petey says.

"Please don't," Lizbet says.

Petey clears the glass and winks. "He made me promise to tell him immediately if you ever came in. I'll be back in a few seconds to make you another cocktail. I assume you'd like another?"

"You betcha," Lizbet says.

Petey vanishes into the back for just an instant, then returns to shake up the second Heartbreaker. (*Breaker, not broken!* Lizbet thinks.) Tony Bennett is replaced by Elvis Costello singing "Alison." *I know this world is killing you.* Lizbet focuses on being present. She is, finally, *out.* It's a hurdle cleared. And not only is she out, but she's at the Blue Bar! She runs her hands over the blue granite and admires how the late-afternoon sun catches the bright penny-sheathed wall; she looks for the ceiling panel that conceals the disco ball. The curved banquette upholstered in sapphire velvet would be a wonderful place to curl up and cry.

Maybe JJ and Christina will get married and have six kids and two Labradoodles, and JJ will coach football at the Boys and Girls Club and win citizenship awards, while Lizbet...what will Lizbet do? Work the front desk at a hotel that will receive a three- or possibly even two-key rating from Shelly Carpenter because the hotel is cursed or haunted or both—and that's only if Shelly deigns to show up.

No, Lizbet won't mope. She won't engage in negative thinking. She tries to recall an inspirational meme, but the only one that comes to mind is the quote attributed to Socrates, and she's sick of it.

Lizbet is careful to just sip her second cocktail. The strawberry and ginger and blood orange square-dance on her palate—spiraling out, reeling back in. She closes her eyes.

"It's good, right?" Petey says. "Those strawberries were picked at Bartlett's Farm this morning."

"Did you tell Chef I was here?" Lizbet asks.

"I sure did."

"Is he coming out?"

"Coming out here?" Petey says.

Yes, Lizbet thinks. That's what chefs do when there's a VIP— they come out to the dining room to say hello. It's only a quarter past five, so there's no way Mario is in the weeds yet.

"He doesn't believe in it," Petey says.

Lizbet feels stung; it's another rejection—not that she cares one whit about Mario Subiaco. He's full of himself.

She should probably leave. Even in 2022, there's something a little pathetic about a woman sitting at a bar alone. Lizbet has a bottle of Krug champagne at home, languishing in the back of her fridge. She'll drink the whole thing by herself. She was saving it for a monumental occasion, either good or bad. She had hoped, of course, for the former and gotten the latter, but there's no denying that Christina taking over Lizbet's job at the Deck is monumental.

Petey disappears into the back again and Lizbet can't blame her for wanting to escape; Lizbet isn't exactly a fountain of scintillating conversation. When Petey returns, she's holding a silver julep cup lined with parchment and filled with golden, crispy, paper-thin potato chips. Alongside these, she sets a dipping sauce that looks like creamy Thousand Island flecked with herbs.

"Our amnesia sauce," she says. "It's so good, it makes you forget everything else."

Oh, but that this were true, Lizbet thinks. Then she tastes it—and for one sublime moment, she can't remember her own name, much less the name of her ex-boyfriend or the wine rep he was sexting. For the next few minutes, she exists in a bubble where it's only her, the Heartbreaker, the blue granite, and the world's best chips and dip.

Elvis Costello yields to Van Morrison, "Crazy Love." The playlist isn't helping her, but what does help is Petey appearing with a trio of deviled eggs, one topped with bacon, one sprinkled with snipped chives, the third crowned with diced sweet red pepper. Lizbet takes a bite of each. They're perfection. If Lizbet closes her eyes, she could swear she was back in Minnetonka at the annual First Lutheran...

"Chef calls these his church-picnic eggs," Petey says.

Yes, precisely.

"Another Heartbreaker?" Petey asks.

"You betcha!" When Lizbet drinks, she starts sounding *very* Minnesota. "Please and thank you." She'll Uber home if she has to. Other people have entered the bar and are tucked into the banquettes. Lizbet doesn't know anyone—yet. The second she sees a familiar face, she'll leave.

The third Heartbreaker arrives along with three chilled soup shooters—curried zucchini, cream of Vidalia onion, and a spicy watermelon gazpacho. Behind that are two hot chicken sliders with house-made pickles and cafeteria tacos, which are like the ones Lizbet remembers from Clear Springs Elementary except the shells are crispier, the ground beef richer, the shredded cheese smokier, the tomatoes riper, and the iceberg crunchier. Lizbet takes a bite of this, a nibble of that. She watches sausages wrapped in puff pastry with some kind of mustard sauce go past her and she feels a pang of envy. She'll get that next time, along with the painterly array of miniature vegetables from Pumpkin Pond Farm, served with buttermilk ranch. The food is so fresh and so fun and so flawlessly presented that Lizbet decides Mario Subiaco can have all the bragging rights he wants. The music picks up energy—Counting Crows, Eric Clapton. Lizbet bobs her head along. She hasn't looked at her phone even once; she is not unproud of that. She's a woman having fun at a bar alone. What was she afraid of?

Beatriz appears behind the bar, holding a tray of chilled shot glasses.

"Here's our whipped cream concierge," Petey says.

Whipped cream concierge! The third Heartbreaker has gone to Lizbet's head and she gives a little shriek. What a gifted idea!

"Our flavors tonight are coconut and caramel apple," Beatriz says. "Would you like one?"

"You *betcha!*" Lizbet says. "One of each, please and thank you!"

Beatriz arranges the shot glasses in front of her and hands her a demitasse spoon. Lizbet starts with the coconut, which tastes like a mouthful of coconut cloud, then moves to the caramel apple.

A man takes a seat two over from Lizbet. "Hey, hot stuff," he says to her, extending a hand. "I'm Brad Dover from Everett."

"Hi?" Lizbet says. Brad Dover has a thick Southie accent and a meaty face and, no doubt, a closet filled with Bruins jerseys and a bone to pick with Tom Brady.

He turns to Petey. "I'd like an Irish car bomb, please, dollface."

The only problem with the Blue Bar, Lizbet decides, is that it's open to the public, including people like Brad Dover from Everett, men who order Irish car bombs and call complete strangers "dollface" and "hot stuff." It's definitely time for her to go.

"I'll take my check, please and thank you," she says.

Petey raises her palms. "Everything is on the house."

"You're kidding," Lizbet says. "Well, thank you, it was extraordinary."

"You can't leave yet," says Brad Everett from Dover—or is it Brad Dover from Everett? She neither knows nor cares. "I just got here."

Exactly, she thinks. She pulls out two twenties to leave for Petey as a tip, swivels away from Brad Dover, and comes face-to-face with the person who has taken the seat on the other side of her, and that person is Mario Subiaco. He's in a white chef's jacket and a White Sox cap, and he's a little sweaty, which only serves to make him even hotter than she remembers.

"Hey there, Heartbreaker," he says.

She reels back in surprise. "I thought you didn't come out of the kitchen."

"There's an exception to every rule," he says. "How was your food?"

"It was...it was..."

"That good?" he says.

"Better than that good," she says—and to her mortification, she feels tears gathering. It's the vodka, obviously; she's had three Heartbreakers in just over an hour—who does that? A woman who is eating out for the first time in months, a woman who has had her shoddily stitched-up heart ripped apart at the seams *again*. It's not Christina's gloating that's making her cry. It's kindness—the food itself and someone caring what she thought of it.

Mario smiles into his lap. "Well, thank you. I know you have high standards, so I was trying my hardest. I wasn't sure about the cafeteria tacos."

Lizbet laughs and discreetly wipes under her eyes. "They were a hell of a lot better than the ones our lunch lady Mrs. MacArthur used to serve up."

"Good, good," Mario says. He clears his throat. "So, listen, I have the night of the fifth off and I was hoping I could take you to dinner."

"Hey, buddy boy," Brad Dover from Everett says. "Buzz off. I'm taking her out."

"No," Lizbet says to Mario. "He's not. And yes, I'd love to have dinner." She grins. There's no point trying to keep her cool, if she ever even had any, because Mario Subiaco is *asking her out,* which is a sentence that should be punctuated by ten exclamation points. "Where shall we go?"

"I was thinking about the Deck," Mario says. "How does that sound to you?"

Ha-ha-ha-ha! Lizbet thinks. Is this happening? Is this *happening?*

"Sounds perfect," she says.

"That's what I wanted to hear," Mario says. "We have a reservation at eight."

12. Graveyard Shift

Grace can't believe it. She can't *believe it!*

It has taken an entire century, but someone is finally doing the digging necessary to arrive at the truth about Grace's death.

This someone isn't Lizbet Keaton, and it isn't Richie Decameron, who showed such enthusiasm about a ghost in his interview and then promptly forgot about it. This someone is eight-year-old Wanda Marsh. Wanda has become, in modern parlance, *obsessed* with the hotel's ghost. Zeke mentioned the ghost in an offhand remark while Wanda was searching for a mystery to solve, and Wanda seized on the topic. She begged Kimber to take her to the Nantucket Atheneum, where she and librarian Jessica Olson dug into the archives of the *Nantucket Standard* and found the article published on August 31, 1922. Jessica made a photocopy for Wanda, who tucked it into the back of her notebook.

CHAMBERMAID DIES IN HOTEL FIRE

Island coroner Wilbur Freeman reported on Monday that there was one fatality in the fire that engulfed the third floor and attic of the Hotel Nantucket. Grace Hadley, age nineteen, a chambermaid at the hotel, perished in her bed, a death that went previously unnoticed because no one—not even the hotel's general manager, Leroy Noonan—realized that Hadley was living in the attic.

"The room she was occupying was an overflow storage closet that she'd managed to outfit with one of the hotel's cots and was using as a bedroom, unbeknownst to anyone on the staff," Noonan said. "Had we known Grace was living up there, we would have informed the Nantucket Fire Department immediately so that they might have tried to rescue her. Grace was known for her quick sense of humor, her willingness to take on even the most arduous tasks, and her dedication. We will mourn her loss."

As reported in our pages last week, the hotel caught fire at two a.m. on Sunday, August 20, following a spirited dinner dance held in the hotel's ballroom. We have now learned that the cause of the blaze was an "errant cigarette of unknown origin." Hotel owner Jackson Benedict and his wife, Dahlia, were asleep in their suite at the hotel; however, both the Benedicts escaped without injury.

Miss Hadley was predeceased by both of her parents and her brother, George Hadley, a commercial fisherman.

Wanda shows the article to her mother (who finds Wanda's interest in Grace's untimely death a bit disquieting), then to Louie (who doesn't understand or care to), then to Zeke (who indulges Wanda and listens to her read the entire article aloud), then to Adam (who doesn't indulge Wanda), and finally to Edie (who suggests that Wanda write an article that Edie will help her submit to the *Nantucket Standard*).

The truth is right there *between the lines!* Grace thinks. No one realized Grace was living in the attic. (*Jack hid her up there!*) Grace was known for taking on the most arduous tasks. (*Working as*

Dahlia Benedict's lady's maid!) The Benedicts had escaped without injury. *(Dahlia set the fire, then ran out of the building!)*

Grace is flattered that Mr. Noonan mentioned her sense of humor. And her dedication. She's dedicated, all right. It's a hundred years later, and she's still here.

On July 2, in the darkest hour of the night, the door to the fourth-floor storage closet creaks open, and Grace—who isn't asleep, who never sleeps, never rests, though it's all she wants, please, someday—sees Wanda poke her little blond head in.

"Grace?" she whispers.

Oh, for heaven's sake, Grace thinks. *Be careful what you wish for.*

"Are you here, Grace?" Wanda asks.

Yes, sweet child, Grace thinks. *Now go back to bed.*

"Can you give me a sign?" Wanda asks. "Can you…knock?"

Grace considers this. She *can* knock—but what if this leads to trouble? What if it makes Lizbet *actually* hire an exorcist? Wanda might *think* she wants Grace to knock, but when Grace *does* knock, Wanda might scream, faint, or be scarred for life.

There is, apparently, no one more persistent than an eight-year-old.

"Please, Grace?"

Fine, Grace thinks. She knocks, three short, matter-of-fact raps that cannot be mistaken for anything other than the supernatural.

Wanda drops her pad and pencil and claps her hand over her mouth.

Now I've gone and done it, Grace thinks.

Wanda whispers, "I knew it. Thank you, Grace!"

Grace follows Wanda back to her room. Wanda takes the elevator all the way down to the level where the wellness center is and creeps up the back stairs. So *this* is how she avoids the lobby!

Wanda opens the door to suite 114 with the key card she has tucked into her notebook and returns quietly to bed. Tonight she has chosen the lower bunk closest to the door, and Louie is on the upper bunk farthest from the door. Clever girl.

Grace is tempted to pull the covers up over Wanda's shoulders and tuck her in, but she's done enough for one night. She whisks out of the suite and down the corridor. In the lobby—oh, hello!— she finds Wanda's mother, Kimber, leaning over the desk, deep in conversation with Richie. It's so late that Raoul, the night bellman, has gone home. Richie and Kimber are the only two people awake in the entire hotel; this, Grace can sense. They're eating bowls of soft-serve ice cream that Richie has obviously brought from the break room.

"Craig told me I was too critical," Kimber says. "He claimed I was always harping on things that other people—such as my nanny—let ride. Do you know what happens when you let things ride? Mediocrity." She draws a spoon over the melting ridge of chocolate, then holds the spoon in the air before her mouth. "What about you? Is there a Mrs. Richie?"

"I'm divorced," Richie says. "Three kids. Unfortunately, we split while I was still at the insurance company, so my alimony and child-support payments are calculated on an income I no longer make. I worked for a start-up sneaker concern when I left insurance, but my CEO was a twenty-two-year-old kid out of West Hartford whose parents were bankrolling him. He mismanaged the business and it went under."

"Ugh," Kimber says.

"Big ugh," Richie says. "I've tried to go back to court but I still owe my attorney money from the first go-round, so he's not exactly eager to take my calls. I'm way behind in paying Amanda and she refuses to let me see the kids until I catch up."

"Oh no," Kimber says. "I'm so sorry."